My House Gathers Desires

My House Gathers Desires

STORIES BY

Adam McOmber

AMERICAN READER SERIES, NO. 28

BOA EDITIONS, LTD. ❖ ROCHESTER, NY ❖ 2017

First Edition
17 18 19 20 7 6 5 4 3 2 1

For information about permission to reuse any material from this book,
please contact The Permissions Company at www.permissionscompany.
com or e-mail permdude@gmail.com.

Publications by BOA Editions, Ltd.—a not-for-profit cor-
poration under section 501 (c) (3) of the United States
Internal Revenue Code—are made possible with funds
from a variety of sources, including public funds from
the Literature Program of the National Endowment
for the Arts; the New York State Council on the Arts,
a state agency; and the County of Monroe, NY. Private
funding sources include the Lannan Foundation for
support of the Lannan Translations Selection Series;
the Max and Marian Farash Charitable Foundation; the Mary S. Mulligan
Charitable Trust; the Rochester Area Community Foundation; the Steeple-
Jack Fund; the Ames-Amzalak Memorial Trust in memory of Henry
Ames, Semon Amzalak, and Dan Amzalak; and contributions from many
individuals nationwide. See Colophon on page 160 for special individual
acknowledgments.

Cover Art: Sandy Knight/Josh Hoffman
Cover Design: Sandy Knight
Interior Design and Composition: Richard Foerster
Manufacturing: McNaughton & Gunn
BOA Logo: Mirko

Library of Congress Cataloging-in-Publication Data

Names: McOmber, Adam, author.
Title: My house gathers desires / Adam McOmber.
Description: First edition. | Rochester, NY : BOA Editions Ltd., 2017. |
    Series: American readers series ; no. 28
Identifiers: LCCN 2017010672 (print) | LCCN 2017013313 (ebook) | ISBN
    9781942683421 (eBook) | ISBN 9781942683414 (softcover : acid-free paper)
Subjects: | BISAC: FICTION / Short Stories (single author). | FICTION /
    Fantasy / Historical. | FICTION / Literary.
Classification: LCC PS3613.C58645 (ebook) | LCC PS3613.C58645 A6 2017
(print)
    | DDC 813/.6—dc23
LC record available at https://lccn.loc.gov/2017010672

BOA Editions, Ltd.
250 North Goodman Street, Suite 306
Rochester, NY 14607
www.boaeditions.org
A. Poulin, Jr., Founder (1938–1996)

Contents

My House Gathers Desires

Hydrophobia

The lake was a dark spill among the trees. Forked branches broke the surface of the water, carving ripples in the shallows. Shingles curled in the edge weeds along the ribbed and sandy shore. Going to the lake became part of Jane's routine while Scott was at clinic. She put on a sundress and made her way down the rocky path behind the rental house, listening to the ratcheting sound of birdsong and the churn of the distant refinery. It wasn't until the boy appeared on the other side of the lake that Jane realized just how restless she'd become. She watched him pick his way, barefoot, down the path. He wore a white cotton shirt and a pair of old-fashioned woolen pants rolled to a place above his ankles. With him, he carried a sheaf of paper and a leather roll that Jane soon discovered contained paintbrushes and a set of watercolors. The boy propped his paper against a rock and took a tin cup to the edge of the lake. His black hair fell across his forehead as he bent to dip the cup into the water, and when he rose, he looked at Jane. She lifted her hand. He lifted his hand in return. Then the boy began his work.

Jane thought it was charming for a child so young—no more than ten or eleven—to be so intent on making art.

This boy was a picture of silence, nothing like the sons and daughters of her friends in the city. She returned to her reading and stopped only when she felt the boy watching her. Jane looked up. The boy didn't smile. "Are you always going to be here now?" he called. She realized the lake had probably been his place for making art long before she'd come along and ruined his solitude.

"Am I—" Jane searched for the right word, "trespassing?"

"I'm just wondering," he said.

"I like it here," Jane said.

He glanced at the plastic soda bottle that leaned against her hip. "Do you think you could bring me one of those drinks tomorrow?"

She laughed. His tone was so serious. "I can go back to the house and get one now if you'd like."

"Tomorrow," he said.

"Tomorrow then," Jane replied.

That evening Scott barely spoke when he returned from clinic. He turned on the television. They watched the only station available, a Christian network, washed in static. A blond woman in a gaudy silk dress talked about a personal experience she'd had with Satan.

"Do you want to watch a movie?" Jane asked.

"That's okay," her husband replied, yawning. "I'm exhausted."

They continued to watch as the woman described a visitation in her bedroom several years before. Satan had come to stand at the foot of the woman's bed. In his presence, she could not move her limbs. She could not use her voice. He leered at her with strange bright eyes. She said the eyes seemed to echo with a terrible sound.

The next day, Jane brought two diet cherry sodas to the lake along with a bag of pretzels. After placing them on her picnic blanket, she waited. An hour went by. Jane kept the book open in her lap but didn't read. She glanced frequently at the path across the lake. The boy didn't appear. As the day wore on and the heat and insects intensified, Jane understood he likely wasn't coming. She killed a fly on her calf and decided to go home.

When Jane returned to the rental house, she realized how long she'd stayed at the lake. Scott's car was already in the drive. He sat at the kitchen table looking over some work, barely glancing at her when she came through the mudroom door. "Thirsty?" he said, taking brief notice of the two soda bottles.

Jane almost told him about the boy, but decided against it. "It gets hot out there," she said, returning the unopened soda to the refrigerator and tossing the other into the recycling bin.

"Did you take your mace?" Scott asked.

The question surprised her. He'd never mentioned the canister of mace that she carried on her key chain before.

"You should take it," he said. "And your phone. If you got a look at some of the guys I see—" Scott shook his head.

The next day, the boy was already at the lake when Jane arrived. Copper-colored clouds crowded the sky, threatening a storm. Jane raised the two soda bottles so he could see. She was glad she'd decided to bring both of them again. The boy went back to painting for a moment, applying strokes to an unseen work. Then he stood, dusted off his pants and started to make his way around the lake. The wind pushed his black hair over his eyes. He didn't bother to push it away. It was as if he didn't need to see. Perhaps he used some form of echolocation, Jane mused, like a bat. When the boy was close, an idea came to her. It was as if the idea had surfaced from the murky lake itself. Jane realized the boy was the type of son she wanted. A quiet one who painted pictures. A child full of interesting thoughts. She felt a twinge of pain at this.

The boy took the soda from her, and after a moment of studying the twist-off cap, turned it, releasing a hiss of air. He took a drink and seemed vaguely surprised. "What is this?" he asked.

"It's diet," Jane said. "I'm sorry."

The boy lifted the bottle to study the carbonated liquid inside. Then he returned his gaze to Jane. "What's that you're reading," he asked, pointing to the book on the blanket. He had a faint accent. Though what sort of accent it was, Jane couldn't be sure.

"Poetry," she said. "Old poetry."

After another long drink, he said, "Can I look?"

"I doubt you'd like it. It's not really the sort of thing I like either. I found it at the house." Jane thought of a line from one of the poems: *Joy's recollection is no longer joy, while sorrow's memory is sorrow still.* It struck her that she'd been recollecting joy for so long, at least since she and Scott had moved to Hollansburg, she'd almost forgotten what it was to actually experience that emotion. And sorrow? She didn't want to think about sorrow.

The boy studied the book's cover. It showed a haunted landscape. Black craggy hills rose from a curling mist.

"Is that the kind of thing that you paint?" Jane asked.

He shook his head. "I paint water."

"You mean you paint the lake?"

"Just water," he said.

"Do you want to sit?" she asked.

"I should go back. Ma will be looking for me."

"Does your family live close by?"

The boy glanced over his shoulder. "What color would you say the water is today?"

"Oh, I don't know," she said. "Sort of gray? Gloomy. It's probably going to storm."

For a moment, the boy grew silent. "I think it looks red," he said finally.

She cleared her throat. "Really?" There was nothing red about the water.

"I should go," he said. He extended the bottle that was still almost full of soda. "Should I give this back?"

"Oh no," Jane said. "You can drink the rest."

He started away and then looked at her again. The sun came through the storm clouds and made his black hair look even darker. "You live at the house near the end of the path, don't you?" he said, pointing in the direction of the rental house.

"That's right," Jane said.

He nodded. "That's called the Miner's House."

"No one's ever told us that," she said.

"A miner and his wife used to live there. She got sick."

"Oh?"

"She died," the boy said. He paused. "I have to go."

That night, as Jane lay in bed, she watched a shaft of moonlight move across the ceiling. She thought about the words the boy had spoken: "She got sick. She died." Jane almost felt as if she could hear the boy speaking still. She wondered if the miner's wife had lain sick in this very room. Scott told her once that, for many years, people in this area had suffered at home. The closest hospital was forty miles away. "We hear stories," Scott said. "Kitchen surgeries and—"

"Scott," Jane had said. "Don't."

"Then there's the cough," he continued. "The old miners can't catch their breath."

Jane pictured the big men down in the stony darkness. She pictured their wives waiting for them to come home.

"I'm glad I'm here," Scott said. "To help."

The next day, the boy brought two pieces of bread wrapped in a dirty towel and offered one to Jane. "Ma makes these," he said.

She took the bread that was round and flat, something like a host at church. "Tell your mother I said thank you."

"She doesn't know about you," he said. He drank his soda, and Jane wondered if he ever changed his clothes. The pants he wore were stained. It looked like he'd been crawling in the dirt. There were buttons where suspenders were meant to fasten. One of the buttons was missing.

"What color is the lake today?" she asked.

"It's black," he said, "and really hard to paint."

"Interesting," Jane replied.

"You're just saying that," he said, "because you don't understand."

"That's true, I suppose."

"If you understood, you'd want to paint the lake yourself."

"Maybe one day," she said.

"I don't remember the miner's name," the boy said, as if they'd already been talking about this subject. "He was a good man though. Then his wife got sick. That turned him into a bad man. Desperate. You know how that can happen?"

She said she did without thinking. The boy had a surprisingly adult manner of speaking.

"One wrong thing," the boy said, shaking his head. "They took him away. Locked him up."

"What kind of illness did the miner's wife have?"

The boy nursed his diet soda. "She was afraid of light. Got bit by an animal in the yard. Couldn't tell anyone what kind of animal it was either. She said it came up out of the earth. She repeated that again and again. The bite swelled as big as an apple, and she couldn't bear to go out in the sun. Pretty soon, even a low-burning fire was too much light. She craved water. Couldn't get enough. Her skin turned a horrible color."

"Was the animal rabid?" Jane said.

The boy shrugged. "They built her a second house where she could live away in the dark. Your house is the miner's house. The wife's house," the boy pointed toward the woods on the other side of the lake, "is over there."

"Did her husband visit her?" Jane said.

"He went once or twice a week," the boy said, "to check if she was still alive. He hoped she wasn't. But somehow, she always was, lying there underneath a bunch of blankets. He could see her shifting restlessly, breathing. So one day, the miner decided he was going to kill his wife. He understood she must be in a state of terrible misery. And if she wouldn't die right, he knew he had to help her along. He got his shotgun—took it down to the wife's house in the cave. He walked straight through the door, up to the pile of blankets that was rising and falling."

"Yes—"Jane said, waiting.

"He got his gun ready. He knew he'd have to shoot

her quick or he wouldn't be able to do it at all. Even he wasn't *that* bad a man. If he saw her face too long, he might remember she'd worn flowers for him at their wedding. He might remember the first time they'd kissed. He took a big handful of the blanket and yanked it back, ready to pull the trigger. But what he saw underneath was something else. His old wife was already dead, had been for months by the look of things. What had been making the blanket move up and down were animals. They'd made nests in her body—in her hollowed out chest and in her guts. Some of them even had young ones inside her."

Jane felt sick. "Who told you a story like that?"

"No one," he said. "I picked it up, bits and pieces. It's the kind of thing that's known around here."

"Well, it's probably not true," Jane said. "It's—I don't know—it sounds like something that bored, unpleasant people would think up."

The boy let his empty soda bottle fall to the grass. Its plastic shone in the sunlight. "I didn't mean offense," he said. "You wanted to hear."

"It was just a scary story, that's all," Jane said. "It's fine."

"The house is still there," he said. "In the cave."

"Now you *are* making things up."

"I can show you."

Jane looked at his pale, narrow face. "I don't think I want to see something like that.

The boy smoothed his black hair with one hand. "I have to go."

"What?"

"I didn't get to paint the lake today," he said. "Maybe tomorrow." He dusted off his worn pants. "Do you care if

I drink the rest of your soda? It doesn't look like you're going to finish."

She handed him her bottle, and without saying thank you, he walked toward the other side of the lake to collect his painting kit. Watching him, Jane wondered if she could ever come back to the lake after hearing such a story as the one he'd told.

Jane and Scott watched television again that night. The image was bathed in milk-white static. The woman in the gaudy silk dress handed out dolls to sick children. She gave a sermon on demons. She said it was important never to converse with one. That was how demons gained their power. "Rebuke them," she said. "Cast them out as soon as they reveal themselves."

Scott stood up and turned the television off. He led Jane to the bedroom where they had a sleepy sort of sex.

The next morning, before Jane was finished with her bowl of cereal, she realized she would, of course, return to the lake. What else did she imagine she'd do with her day? She walked down the wooded path, grabbing at branches and watching the morning light move in the canopy of leaves. She'd put on tennis shoes when normally she would have worn sandals. When she arrived at the shore, she found the boy not painting but sitting on her side of the lake with a canvas in his lap. She realized she'd forgotten to bring a soda for him. He seemed unhappy about this, but only for a moment. He said, "I made a picture for you. To show you it's real."

"A picture?" Jane said.

The boy turned his canvas toward her and held it so she could see. Toothy faces peered up out of the charcoal black. A human figure lay at the center of a roiling cluster of animals. The figure was crudely rendered, but Jane understood it was meant to be a woman. Hairy creatures curled inside her body. The tiny head of one emerged from her open mouth.

"She wasn't the miner's wife anymore, you see?" the boy said. "She was the mother of the animals by then."

The image made Jane's stomach turn. It was the kind of sickness that required action. She needed to know the boy's story wasn't true. "I'll go with you," she said, "to the wife's house in the cave."

The boy dropped the painting into the grass. "I knew you would."

Suddenly, Jane wondered if she should just take this boy away with her. She could run far from Hollansburg. They could travel south. She'd protect the boy from all the awfulness he'd clearly been subjected to in this place.

The boy was already pulling her toward his side of the lake.

Jane allowed herself to be led.

His path was darker than her own. Eventually, it grew so narrow and leafy that Jane worried it wouldn't take them anywhere at all. But the boy diverged from the path before the trees swallowed it entirely. Jane caught a glimpse of an opening in the earth. "Be careful," the boy said. "It's dark. And there are bats living in there."

"Bats?" Jane said.

But there wasn't time for questions. The boy moved quickly now.

Together they passed out of the wooded light and into the cave, which was indeed so dark that Jane couldn't see her own body. She had to trust that the boy would lead her in the right direction. "Stop here," he said in the darkness. He let go of Jane's hand. She felt the coldness of the cave touch every part of her. She wished she hadn't worn her sundress.

The cave brightened then, and the boy emerged from behind two rocks. He held an antique oil lantern with the wick trimmed low. "This lamp is like what the miners used," he said. "Back when the mines were still working. I found it."

Jane looked up at the ceiling of the cave. The craggy surface appeared to be alive, undulating. The boy was right. There were bats.

"Come on," he said.

Again, she allowed him to lead her. Eventually the cave widened into a kind of high dark chamber. In the shadows, she saw a small wooden shack, hastily constructed, nail heads pushing free. Two glassless windows bracketed a makeshift door that leaned against its frame.

"If you look inside, you'll see her bed," the boy said.

When he let go of her hand, Jane suddenly wondered why she'd allowed him to bring her down here. She was from the city. She was a professor's daughter. A doctor's wife. Things hadn't been right in her life for some time. That much was true. But she could make them better. She and the boy should have remained together in the sunlight. She could have explained to him how to stay safe in the woods. "I don't want to go any further," she said. "We need to go back."

The boy's face glowed white in the lamplight. His eyes looked nearly silver. "The miner's wife liked the dark," he said, "craved it. This was the only place for her."

"She should have seen—" Jane paused, thinking the word "doctor." But she couldn't speak it.

"Just come see." The boy ran ahead and was already

pushing at the wooden door of the little house, using all his strength. He motioned for her to come, and Jane walked toward the dark doorway, almost as if she was in a dream. The light from the boy's lantern allowed her to see a filthy blanket piled on a broken bedframe. The mattress beneath was torn and gnawed. She pictured the miner's wife, wretched with sickness, moaning for water.

"I've always been afraid to check and see if there's anything under the blanket," the boy said. "Can you look for me?"

Jane didn't want to look. Yet she knew she'd dream about this house. And it would be better to dream of an empty bed than one still full of a poor woman's corpse. Jane went to what she thought might be the head of the broken bed, the part furthest from the door. Gingerly, she touched the blanket, reaching beneath it. She felt something furry and warm. Something that twitched. Then there was pain, bright searing pain in the meat of her hand, between her thumb and index finger. Jane jerked back and saw blood. She'd been bitten by something beneath the blanket. Something with terrible sharp teeth. She screamed. She couldn't help herself. Then came the sound of leathery wings. Bats seemed to come from everywhere at once, flooding the little house, striking the walls. Jane flailed at the bats, knocking them from the air. The boy dropped the lantern. The house went dark.

Jane awoke to find the boy curled next to her in the cave. The pain was no longer confined to her bleeding hand. It had spread up her arm, into her chest. She felt strange. It felt as if the bats had flown into her body and now clung to her insides, shuddering there. She gathered the boy. He was so small, so pale. Making her way out of the cave, she coughed at the dust caught in her throat and then spat. The boy stirred but didn't wake.

Night had fallen, and it was difficult to see in the dark. She could only make out the shapes of trees. The smell of the woods helped her navigate. She carried the boy back to the lake. The water at night was neither blue nor gray. It was somehow gold, a shifting royal color that moved in molten currents. Putting the boy down beside his easel rock, she went to the lake and rather than cupping her hand to lift the golden water to her mouth, Jane got on all fours and drank. She could still feel the bats crawling inside her, moving their stiff, clawed wings.

It was late by the time she arrived at the rental house. Scott's car was parked in the drive. Jane made her way up the littered path, crunching debris beneath her tennis shoes. She wanted to crawl on her hands and knees. She wanted to be closer to the earth. Yet she compelled herself to walk. There were things to take care of here. Things she needed to do. She opened the mudroom door. Scott stank of tonics from his clinic. She could hear how he shifted his papers at the kitchen table.

"Janey," he called. "Is that you? You had me worried."

Jane stood in the shadow of the doorframe. She watched her husband and thought of the cave. She thought of its sorrow.

Scott rose from the table. "Jane, what happened?"

"I—" she said. But what she wanted to say was "we." *We have been in the dark. We have seen the other house—*

Jane felt the bats shift inside her. She was so full of their small wriggling forms.

Scott took a step toward her. "Your face," he said.

Jane thought of the woman in the gaudy silk dress

on the television, the one who handed out dolls to children. That woman didn't understand demons. Jane crossed her arms over her chest. She shivered. *We will speak to you from the water,* she thought, *and from the very depths of the earth. When we speak, you will listen. And you will come to care for us. We are that which is meant to be cared for.*

"Are you cold?" Scott said. "My God, Jane."

She hadn't asked the boy if the miner and his wife had a son, but she knew now they did. They'd had a quiet son who painted pictures. She wondered what trials he'd been through after his mother and father were both taken from him. How long had he suffered alone? How long had he wandered?

Jane understood she needed to prepare the house. For soon, the boy would wake. He'd walk up the weedy path from the lake. He wouldn't hurry. Jane pictured him in his ragged clothes, eyes of forged silver. It was as if his eyes were mined from the earth itself. The boy wanted to feel safe. He wanted to come home.

Scott was closer now. He looked confused, frightened.

He couldn't be here when the boy arrived. Jane understood that. She thought of the cave once more: the wife's house, the mother's house. Her jaw felt tight. Her teeth, too big.

Scott reached for her.

Jane opened her mouth.

Petit Trianon

"If only Eleanor and I had remained in Paris that day," Anna Moberly writes in an unsent letter to her sister, datcd October 3, 1901, "our lives would not have been altered. Not in such an unnatural way, at least. I would still be with my dear girl now, holding her as I once did." The letter, along with two calfskin diaries filled with notes written in the finely looped cursive of a schoolteacher, was recently discovered in an archive of the St. Hugh's School at Oxford. (*Have the dead suddenly begun to dream?* a page in one of the diaries asks. *Or have they been dreaming all along? And is it possible to become ensnared in such a dream like a gull in a fisherman's net?*) Moberly, a venerable matron, acted as headmistress at the girls' school for some eleven years. She was said, at times, to walk the marble halls with an appearance of such loneliness that even the sunniest of girls were made to feel melancholy. Her gaze was always searching, looking for something that did not appear to exist. And then one day, the headmistress found Eleanor Jardin, an elegant young woman from Somerset. How the two women met is a story lost to history. What is better known, of course, is that Jardin soon became Moberly's assistant. The two began a secret affair in February of 1900, meeting once or twice a week in a small rented room near the school. It's said they created a world together in that room, quietly serving tea and reading books of poetry. For a time, they lived as any husband and wife. Yet they were quiet about their actions, so as not to be too harshly judged.

Their trip to Paris in late August of 1901 was meant to provide an extended romantic escape, a time for the two women to be more fully at ease. Moberly's letter to her sister sheds new light, not on the affair itself, but on the now infamous incident—often dismissed as a *folie à deux*—experienced at the Palace of Versailles. It's well known that both women provided an account of the events after their separation. But the newly discovered letter reveals details far more disconcerting than anything in the official reports.

"Eleanor had taken up a recent interest in the history of the Revolution," Moberly writes, "and despite the heat of late summer, my young friend persisted in her wish to visit the palace. She said she wanted to see how the king and queen had lived before their imprisonment and execution. The kind of life that Madame de la Tour du Pin had called a 'laughing and dancing toward the precipice.' And who was I to refuse my darling girl?

"Versailles itself, we soon discovered, was in a state of dreadful disrepair—looking more like a poorly painted stage set than a monument of historical significance. We walked together through the Halls of Venus and of Mars, the Blue Dining Room where the court had once taken dinner, and the narrow apartments belonging to the servants. As evening came on, I said we shouldn't tarry. We should make our way into the garden. Perhaps there we'd find a more picturesque setting. Eleanor and I went arm in arm through the great doors of the Mirror

Gallery, like two girls from a novel."

Moberly writes that young Eleanor looked lovely in the dying light, auburn hair pulled into a loose bun and her gray dress so fresh and soft. As the two of them progressed, Eleanor perched a pair of spectacles on the bridge of her nose and read aloud from *The Baedecker Guidebook*: "'On your left,' she said, 'are the remains of the King's Labyrinth, populated by bronzed statues and hidden fountains. And just ahead is Marie Antoinette's famed refuge, Petit Trianon—a structure, designed initially for Louis XV's mistress, Madame de Pompadour, which Antoinette quickly made her own. The young queen constructed marvelous follies in the Trianon Gardens: a rustic farm village with actors playing the roles of peasants, a false mountain where goats could graze, and a carousel of porcelain farm animals. It is said that, when she was imprisoned, the queen often wept when she thought of Trianon. The whole of it, she said, was such a foolish dream.'

Moberly continues, "Both Eleanor and I paused there on the stony path, for though we saw the remnants of the King's Labyrinth, we did not see any sign of Petit Trianon or its itinerant follies. Eleanor said we must have simply missed the 'little palace,' though I could not imagine how. I was aware that Petit Trianon, despite its name, was an imposing structure—a grand neoclassical temple, complete with Corinthian columns and intricate rococo moldings. The guidebook was most certainly mistaken in regards to the whereabouts of the building. But because I knew a search would please my Eleanor, I said we should retrace our steps and look for the little palace. 'Circle 'round,' were the exact words I used. I've wondered since if that phrase might have acted as an incantation, causing the natural order of things to shift. For isn't it true that mages often draw circles in the sand to complete some spell? And don't witches too arrange themselves in circles on their Sabbat?

"Not some twenty paces after we'd made our circle, a lone female figure emerged from the tall hedges of the King's Labyrinth. At first, I believed she was another tourist. Though thinking back on the encounter now, I find it difficult to say why I assumed such a thing. The woman walked with a certain stiffness in her gait. She was dressed in a pale and outdated garment. The crinoline of her gown had yellowed with age. Her white-blond hair was bound in a loose braid. And she had a somber air about her. I did not see her face at first. Or if I did, I don't recall.

"I remember thinking I should say something to the woman. Perhaps make an apology, as Eleanor and I had been laughing a bit too loudly only a moment before. But I didn't have time to speak, as my dearest Eleanor was then pulling at me. She sensed something was amiss before I did. Maybe it was her study of the Revolution that gave her a clue. Or maybe it was simply because Eleanor so often understood things better than I. She knew, for instance, that our little apartment at Oxford would never last. Such dreams, she told me, they can't go on. One must always awaken. 'Come, Anna,' she said in the garden. 'Walk faster.' But the heels of my boots made it difficult to walk quickly on the gravel path, and I wondered, at any rate, why we needed to hurry in the terrible heat of late August.

"That's when the trees before us began to *change*. I do not rightly know how to describe what occurred. I can only say the transformation didn't happen all at once, but by degrees, until eventually the trees appeared as if they had no thickness. They were flat, like images painted on a tapestry. Fruit hanging from the branches (oranges, I believe) looked not like spheres, but like dabs of color on an aging canvas. I thought I was having an attack in the heat. I gripped Eleanor's arm. 'Just come on, Anna,' she whispered. 'Please. We mustn't let that woman catch up.'

"It was then that the landscape—the flat trees bearing painted fruit—began to *fold*. I perceived what appeared to be a crease forming in the middle distance—a dark line drawing inward among the flattened trees. Eleanor and I were moving *toward* that crease at such a pace, I thought we'd soon be swallowed by it, just as the trees were being swallowed. What lay beyond the fold, I could not imagine.

"Despite Eleanor's pleadings for me not to do so, I looked back. I wanted to know if the woman from the hedge—the white interloper in the ruined gown—still followed us. I hoped she'd given up her pursuit. Certainly, I didn't want to be forced any closer to the odd black fold that had appeared in the landscape ahead.

"And it was then, when I looked back, that I saw the figure's face for the first time. Perhaps Eleanor had seen it earlier. That's why she'd told me to come away. For the face was no proper face at all. Instead, the woman's flesh had a fold in it, like the landscape, a kind of crease running down the center. The figure in the yellowed dress had no eyes. No mouth. Her features were all lost. And still she came for us. Slowly. Deliberately.

"I would learn later that the palace and its gardens were built upon what had once been swampland. Louis XIII had drained the swamp. The ground at Versailles was sacred to him. And I believe now it was the ancient swampland—the environment that preceded Versailles—

that began to seep out of the fold that had formed in the middle-distance. A greenish-black substance, a primordial liquid, appeared to leak, inklike, into the sky and then onto the grounds themselves. Staining all of it. Changing the very nature of things. My own skirts were weighed down by dampness. 'What on earth is this?' I asked Eleanor. 'Some kind of storm?'

"In response, she would only say: 'We've made a mistake, Anna. I don't know how—'

"In later research—trying to make sense of the events of the day—I would learn that, when the executioner cut off the head of Marie Antoinette at the guillotine in the Place de Grève, peasants rushed forward to dip slips of paper into her blood. They wanted the gore as a keepsake. And in this mad jostling, the wooden trough that contained the queen's head was overturned, spilling a quantity of Antoinette's vital fluids into the dirt, creating what was described by one onlooker as a 'terrible dark swamp made of our queen's very essence.'"

Here the handwriting of Moberly's letter becomes increasingly erratic, nearly illegible, before the narrative ends abruptly.

"Sister, my dear," Moberly writes, "it was there in the swamp that we finally discovered the palace we'd been searching for—the queen's Petit Trianon. And I realized, in horror, that the little palace was not lost to history. All of it had come alive again, and it was impossibly transformed. I could see the peasant village Marie Antoinette had built for herself, now a desperate medieval shanty-town replete with dark figures that shifted, humped and strange, through the crooked streets. And there too was the carousel of farm animals hitched to a wheel. They were not made of porcelain as the guidebook suggested. Instead, the animals were all terribly alive. Bones protruded at sharp angles from their flesh, and the beasts called out in pain as they struggled beneath their heavy yokes. On the horizon, a black mountain rose—the queen's mountain—an awful broken shape against the stained gray sky. And then finally, we saw Petit Trianon itself. But this was not the peaceful retreat I'd imagined—no, this was a black and swollen temple with tall reddish windows and terrible figures that moved within—aristocrats in high pale wigs and gilded gowns. These men and women had been tortured, eyes extracted from faces, blood clotting in the powder that lay upon their skin. One man carried his head like a lantern. A woman held a handful of her own broken teeth.

"When we came into view of Petit Trianon, the revenant that pursued us, the walking horror in white, began to call out in a voice unlike any I'd ever heard—a high and unintelligible wail. The grotesqueries in the black palace gathered at the windows to gaze at her. The dead queen behind us—for that is what I believe she was, Marie Antoinette herself, living in the gardens of her own deceased imagination—raised her arms. Her flesh was the color of stone, a petrification of life. She called to her court. She screamed for them.

"It was only a few steps more before I stumbled, falling into a damp low place in the earth. I thought for certain I was finished. The queen's court would pour from Petit Trianon. They would fall upon me. When Eleanor turned to help, I told her she must go. She must hurry on. Make her way out of this infernal place. She did as I asked, blind with fear, and the dead queen followed, pallid arms outstretched.

"Hours later, I finally found my beloved girl. Eleanor was still drenched in the black waters of the swamp. Her limp body was curled in the shadows beneath a lemon tree, face pressed against its trunk. We were on the outskirts of the grounds; the garden had seemingly returned to its previous natural state.

"'Eleanor,' I said, breathlessly. 'What happened, my darling? How did you find safety?'

"Eleanor made no response.

"'We must go back to Paris,' I said. 'We must tell someone what's happened to us.'

"Finally, she turned to look at me, eyes dull. She did not move to leave.

"'My dearest,' I said.

"Eleanor studied my face. It was as if she no longer quite recognized me. 'Tell someone?' she said finally. 'Who would we tell?'

"'Anyone,' I said. 'Anyone who will listen.'

"'Anna,' she whispered. 'We made a mistake—'

"'But we've done nothing *wrong*,' I said. 'We only have to leave the garden. Go back to the city.'

"She shook her head. 'We must pray for the queen,' she said. 'And pray for ourselves. This isn't the sort of dream that lets you go. This is the sort of dream that stays.' And with that, Eleanor pressed her face against the lemon tree, and she looked at me no longer."

Sodom and Gomorrah

We pause at our work and watch as two strangers make their way across the plain. Their flesh is salt-white, covered in chalk from the cliffs near the sea. Their eyes are lamplit, wanting. They ask to wash themselves in the pool at the center of our square. They want to rest in the shade of the standing stone. We understand their desires. The pool is filled with fresh water, replenished by a buried spring. The stone is our mystery, a ruined monument from bygone days. In winter, the stone has a reddish hue; in summer, it reveals flecks of gold. There are those who claim it is perhaps a pillar dragged from the broken gates of Eden. Others say it is a gravestone, marking the burial place of the monster Tiamat. A few even claim the stone is older still. It fell from the high wall that separated the earth from the sky when the black stars of creation still turned in the firmament.

Wind blows about the stone as the strangers arrive. The cracks in its surface seem to sing. Each of us pauses when we hear the song. In our recollection, the stone has never made any such sound. And yet the song is familiar, nonetheless. Lot, tiresome old scribe, leads the strangers to his home at the dusty edge of the city. He washes them there and feeds them. He asks them questions in a labored voice and later tells his wife he believes they are messengers. "From some king in the East?" Lot's wife asks. Her husband does not answer.

We, who have been listening to the song of the stone, understand the strangers are far more than mere messengers. We realize we have been waiting for them all our dull and toilsome lives. That evening, we are compelled to make a circle around the old man's house. Our mouths are open. Our eyes, hollowed. We hear the song of the old stone, drifting toward us from the square. And all of us sing together. Lot offers his daughters to us (two sullen girls in braids), and we know how ridiculous such an offering is. The old man bars the door in an attempt to protect his messengers. Still singing, we break the door down. Inside, we find them, the two strangers who came. There in the candlelight, they look not like men at all. They wear a human skin, as one might wear a cloak on a cold day. They make a sign with their pale hands that tells us where we are to take them.

We fall upon the strangers, bringing them to the monument in the square. On the marble bier near the pool, we come together, clinging to each other's backs. And using all our strength, we begin to form a single body. It's difficult at first. We wrestle and climb. But soon, we are a giant, composed of innumerable, heaving men. There are those of us who act as the body's great arms, and others are its bracing legs. A number of us fall together and form a hard thick phallus. The strangers then are no longer like two men at all. They have undressed themselves, giving up the pretense of skin and becoming a denser part of the air.

We are hungry for them. Ours is a sacred desire that was buried too long in our chests, like some city beneath the sand. Those of us acting as the giant's hips thrust forward, penetrating the dense air. We press inside a strata of deep time, feeling the lush warmth of it. Deeper still we push until, finally, in a haze of rose and blue, we see a garden. An intricate enclosure, rising. We think of Eden and the Grove of Dilmun, but this is neither of those places. Bright waters lap at the garden's shores. We see the stone—the very monument of Sodom—standing there at the center of the garden, strung with flowering vines. It is newly carved, sculpted with scenes that are strange to us. They tell stories of creation. We realize all our old tales have been a lie. The long ago sun touches our skin. There are animals that walk in the shade of the garden and speak warnings to us in odd tongues. The hare, the lion, the serpent, all of them make portents. But we do not listen. We know our aim. We move our great body, pressing against the membrane that seems to surround and support the ancient garden. We rock against the warmth of it.

When finally we find release, our voices rise, words lit by fire. And the air around us is filled with the sudden bright fluid of a new music. Not a hymn, but something that strums the golden strings of the cosmos itself. We bathe in the sound, losing our grips on each other's backs and slipping down into a jumble in the square. The strangers are there among us, once more sewn inside their lovely skins. We are all covered in the liquid that is neither our own sweat nor the dew of the garden, but something brilliant we have made together. Lot makes his way out of the city, frightened old creature. He takes his daughters to a cave where they will live out their days like animals. Lot's wife turns to look back at us, thinking we men are a marvel—a thing that is entirely new. And we men lie together with the strangers, bare and glistening in the shadow of the stone. We finally understand the meaning of our monument's song, the words it has been chanting even when we could not hear: *There are no gods*, it says in its beautiful voice. *And if there are, my friends, believe me: they do not matter.*

Poet and Underworld

Tents rose against the morning sky, their soot-black peaks like woodcuts inked on a vellum scroll. Late-coming mules made their way toward the fair, dragging skiffs loaded with copperware and bolts of fabric. Men from the coast carried horned ocean fish in water-filled leather tanks, and those from the country pushed carts of fragrant cinnamon and cardamom. Drouet moved carefully, concealing herself behind the black trees at the side of the road. Any one of these travelers might know her father, the burgher. If she was caught, she'd be returned to him by a merchant hoping for reward.

On a different morning, Drouet might have climbed to a low-hanging branch and written about the merchants' procession in her Book of Hours. She'd make a record, as her mother taught her long ago. But she found herself unable to concentrate in the high, pale light of the morning. She was tired of the city and tired of her father's strictures. She wanted to feel the hot and busy release of the fair. And she could think of little more than the elm-shadowed butcher's stall where Bledic would be working. The boy was Italian; he'd come north in a caravan along the Roman road. He fumbled his knife when he worked. He gouged flesh and cursed. It was clear that, like Drouet, he longed for escape.

Drouet had been visiting Bledic since the fair began. The last time they'd spoken, he asked if she had money.

"For what purpose?" Drouet said.

"There's something I want to see," Bledic replied. He worked at the piece of meat on the block in front of him with his knife. Even covered in animal's blood, he was so terribly handsome. Drouet thought that if she got any closer to this boy, a tongue of fire might leap from her skull. "They say there's an entrance to hell," he continued, "over at the southern edge of the fair."

Drouet almost laughed at this but stopped herself. As a rule, she did not favor whimsy. Her mother had told her that such conceits were sometimes even dangerous.

Bledic glanced at Drouet. He made a circle in the air with his still wet knife. "Rumors are nothing more than rumors," he said. "I want to see the place for myself."

"I can get money," Drouet said, thinking of the lead coffer her father kept on the stone mantle. It was full of coins. "I'll bring it tomorrow—on one condition."

"Name it."

"You'll take me along," she said, "to Hell."

Bledic grinned at her. He slid his long knife back into the meat.

The fair was like a painted halo, concentric alleyways cut by the radii of stalls. Bledic's butchery was in the western quadrant. Chickens and rabbits struggled before poultrymen's carts. Drouet rounded the column near charred Tannery Gate, stolen coins jingling in the pocket of her dress. The gate had been damaged in a fire ages ago. According to her father, who kept a chronicle of the city, the Devil himself had appeared at the fair in 1188. He walked the grounds in fine clothes and talked kindly to the men selling wares. A day after his visit, a south-bearing wind carried sparks to the thatched rooftops and burned half the fair to the ground. The burgher said it was likely that the Devil would return one day, as he was drawn to places where he had history.

Drouet didn't care about devils. She cared only about Bledic. When she finally reached the butcher's stall that morning, both the jowled master and his handsome apprentice were working on a calf that lay open to the spine on the wooden block. Blood flowed across the grain of the wood. Black flies swarmed the body. The smell was not of death or rot, but rather a clean coppery scent. It was only when the master slipped behind the tattered curtain of the stall to collect some fresh implement that Drouet allowed herself to approach.

Bledic looked up from the animal, hands gloved in shining blood. "The burgher's daughter," he said, as if he hadn't been expecting her.

"Drouet," she countered.

"Why do you always come alone? Don't you have anyone to walk with?"

"I don't," she replied.

"No mother?"

"I have a mistress," she said, "from Paris. My mother is—" For a moment, Drouet saw her mother's body hanging before her, cool and frail. Her deathbed had been suspended on ropes to avoid an infestation of fleas. Light from a high window illuminated dust motes in the air. Drouet's mother smiled. She mouthed the words "my love."

Drouet pulled herself back from the memory. She

reached into the pocket of her dress, removing the coins she'd stolen from her father's box. Bledic looked at the coins, rolling a bit of animal fat between his fingers and finally flicking it to the ground. "Meet me at Tannery Gate in an hour."

She nodded.

"You aren't frightened?" he asked.

Drouet's skin prickled. The sensation did not come from fear.

"Go, before *signore* returns," Bledic said. "He doesn't like me talking to girls."

Drouet did as Bledic asked, moving away through alleyways, back into the maze of stalls. As always after speaking to Bledic, she felt shaken. She walked through the narrow artisan's corridor and thought of meeting him at Tannery Gate. To actually travel with the young apprentice through the fair. How wonderful would that be?

She paused at a table of painted clay dolls of the sort her mother had once made for her. They had molded heads and burlap bodies that were filled with sawdust. She dared to touch the fragile arm of one and the rough-hewn skirt of another, taking pleasure in their simplicity. The doll merchant, a man with one drooping eyelid, was busy attending to another customer and didn't seem to mind her presence. Drouet certainly didn't look the part of a criminal. The dolls themselves wore absent expressions, neither asking for her attention nor rejecting it. Though Drouet had put away her own playthings when her mother died, she found she longed for one of these dolls now. But what would she do with it when the church bells rang? Carry it along for Bledic to see? Should she also wrap herself in swaddling clothes?

The last doll in the row was larger than the others and curious enough to cause Drouet to momentarily forget the butcher's handsome apprentice. The figure was quite unlike all the others. Made with a finer sense of craftsmanship, its features were detailed in such a way as to make the doll seem almost fit for a reliquary. Yet it was not this precision that interested her. It was the fact that clearly, *astonishingly*, the doll resembled Drouet herself. Its hair was the same as her own—hay-colored and held back from the face. Even more remarkably, the doll wore the red cape, stitched at the hem with lilies, that Drouet donned each day for the fair. The way the doll clasped its hands reminded her of the penitent way she often held her own hands when she walked.

Drouet glanced at the doll merchant who was still busy with his customer. Had this man seen her one day and been so enamored with the burgher's daughter that he made a replica of her? She wondered if that was the sort of thing a man might do. Whatever led to its creation, Drouet knew she had to have the doll. It belonged to her, after all. It *was* her. She certainly could not spend the coins she'd taken from her father's box. Bledic needed those coins. So, with great resolve, Drouet simply grabbed the large doll from the counter and then ran as fast as she could into the jostling crowd with the figure's clay head nodding against her chest.

There was a moment when Drouet felt sure she'd be caught. She knocked against another merchant and fell sprawling in the dust. Yet no one came to take her by the shoulder. No one called her a thief. She was still free, though she'd torn her dress and scraped her arm and didn't look as pretty as she'd intended.

In a nook near the cathedral of St. Étienne, Drouet

concealed herself and sat considering the doll. She wished her mother were still alive so she could ask what such a thing might mean. If Bledic fell in love with her, would he also make a copy of her? A bloody Drouet with bones for eyes and gristle for a tongue?

When the bells rang Terce, Drouet dusted off her dress and tucked the doll under her arm. She couldn't very well leave her double there in the shadow of St. Étienne, and though she tried to make the thing appear as unobtrusive as possible, it was much too large and awkward for true concealment. She reached Tannery Gate by way of side alleys, keeping close lookout for the doll merchant who might be searching for her. She found Bledic leaning against a pillar, thumbs tucked in the waistband of his woolen breeches. His eyes widened at the sight of the doll, but he made no disparaging remarks. It seemed that he'd either learned manners or his mind was elsewhere. "The burgher's daughter," he said.

"Drouet," she replied.

"Follow me," Bledic said, turning away from the gate. Drouet hurried to catch up, the doll kicking at her with its sawdust legs, as if in protest. She followed Bledic along the graceful curve of a wooden alleyway, moving deeper into the fair. They passed guilds marked with the symbols of their patron saints. The wheelwrights were gathered beneath a sign painted with the figure of Saint Catherine, who'd broken a torture wheel merely by touching the instrument with her frail hand. There was Saint Magdalena too, who'd washed the feet of Christ with oil. Saint Claire's face loomed above the mirror maker's stand. She'd been too ill to go to the cathedral, and it was said that an image of the Mass had appeared flickering on the wall of her room so that she might watch the service still.

Drouet looked down at the face of the doll she carried. She wondered whether it might be meant as a sacred image. If Drouet was a saint, what was she patron of?

She nearly lost Bledic in the crowd but then found him again. Spots of animal blood were spattered across the back of his linen shirt. She thought they looked like a constellation of stars.

"Where did you say this stall is again?" she asked him.

"At the very edge of the fair," he replied, not glancing at her.

"What's it to be like," she asked, "this entrance to Hell?"

"Dark and wet," he said. "Full of creatures."

"But isn't Hell supposed to be fiery?"

Bledic continued as if he hadn't heard her question. "There are yearly fairs in the underworld too, you know," he said, "more majestic than the one in Troyes. Impossible wares are sold: golden heads that speak ten languages, animals that wear clothing and walk upright, boxes of blood that can give birth to an army on command."

"How do you know these things?" Drouet asked.

Bledic finally glanced back at her. His gold-flecked eyes were nearly more than she could bear. "Because I'm from Rome," he said. "We know all the old stories there."

"My mother once told me that Hell is nothing more than centuries of poetry," Drouet said.

Bledic seemed irritated. "We'll see," he said. He pointed into the distance where Drouet could make out a low wooden structure with two Doric columns that formed a gate. The columns were clearly made of some cheap material and painted to resemble Italian marble. An old merchant slouched on a stool, wrapped in what appeared to be a winding cloth. He'd fallen asleep in the depths of the fabric. The sign nailed above the entrance did not bear the mark of a saint but rather read, "Averno: Entrance to the Under Realms."

"It's a *theater*, Bledic," Drouet said. "Just look at it. There's probably a stage inside with actors dressed as ghosts and devils who'll prance around for us until we're as bored as the old man who sells glimpses of it."

"I watched a man go in last night," Bledic said. "He didn't come out again."

"Bledic—"

"You have the coins?"

They'd drawn nearer the entrance as they talked, and now they stood in front of the sleeping man who had crusts of yellow tears at the corners of his eyes. Drouet reached into the pocket of her dress and felt a sinking in her stomach. The coins were gone. They must have slipped out when she'd fallen after stealing the doll.

Bledic looked astonished, then angry. "You spent the money on that ridiculous toy, didn't you?"

"Of course not," she said.

He lowered his gaze to the doll, the effigy. "Give it to me. Maybe he'll take it as payment."

Drouet clutched the doll, then realized how silly she must look. If she was ever going to escape this city, escape her father, she had to let go of things. She had to act like a woman. Drouet extended the doll carefully toward the sleeping merchant, who was not, in fact, sleeping. He stared at her from beneath half-closed lids. The old man took the doll, touched its hair gently, then its mouth.

Drouet felt a chill.

The old merchant stood from his stool and swung open an iron gate to allow them passage. Drouet followed Bledic down a narrow hall painted with a mural showing high red cliffs. The two of them came to a landing where a wooden boat waited in a man-made stream.

"You see," Bledic said. "It's not a theater."

"It's a show, nonetheless," Drouet said. Yet she felt a new hesitation when she saw the boat. She was no longer quite sure about Bledic either—the way he'd grown angry when he learned she lost the money. She didn't like how he'd forced her to give away the doll. Yet his hands felt strong and good as he helped her into the boat. His touch still thrilled her. As they pushed away from the dock, she wondered what her father would say if he could see her. She smiled briefly at this, thinking how angry he would be.

The boat glided out into darkness, Bledic at the prow and Drouet in the stern. She thought she could hear the rushing sound of the sea in the distance and wondered how such an effect might be achieved. There were more murals that showed bleaker landscapes, populated by thin wraiths.

"Will you hold my hand?" Drouet asked, and Bledic obliged though he appeared far more interested in the darkness ahead. His palm was sticky with the remains of butcher's blood. Still, Drouet clutched it thankfully.

The little river curved once and then again. She felt they were dropping deeper into the earth. The images on the walls grew stranger, sylphs and satyrs dancing. Symbols hovered in the air before the boat, ancient scripts. Finally the river opened onto a small lake. At the center of the lake was an island of trees—not real trees but painted props with stuffed black birds perched on the branches. "A stage," Drouet whispered. "You see?"

"A forest," Bledic replied excitedly, steering the boat toward the island.

43

Together they disembarked. Drouet felt her boots sink into the muddy quagmire at the island's edge. "We should—" she began, wanting to tell him they should go back. But there was such a silencing about this place. The false trees made a kind of chapel. The stuffed black birds were a congregation, eyes of yellow glass.

"Walk a little more with me," Bledic replied. He took Drouet's hand and eased her forward. "Your mother—perhaps we'll see her. Wouldn't that be good?"

"My mother?" Drouet said, confused.

There was something different about Bledic in this darkness. His eyes shone. His lips curled. It was as if he belonged in this place, Drouet thought. Far more so than he belonged at the butcher's stall.

"Bledic," Drouet said, "how—how did you come to work for the butcher?"

He stared ahead, as if he could see something in the far distance.

"How did you take up your trade?" Drouet repeated.

"It was on a lonely road," he replied, "running north from Rome. Cypress trees made deep shadows there. It was the kind of road that seemed to move toward ancient times. The butcher found me there. He lured me onto his cart."

"Lured you?" Drouet said. A fearful thought occurred to her then. What if the butcher had trapped the boy, forced him to learn a trade? And what if Bledic wasn't merely a boy? She'd sensed that all along somehow, hadn't she? Bledic was something more. And now Drouet was foolishly setting him free.

As they walked, Drouet continued to glance back at the tiny rocking boat in the lake until she could no longer see it through the painted trees. The island was much larger than she'd first imagined. Bledic strode ahead now, hurrying toward something unseen. She remembered how he'd described the yearly fairs in the underworld—the talking golden heads and boxes of blood. Was Bledic's body changing in the dark, Drouet wondered. Did the boy grow smaller and more hunched? Did his fingernails lengthen and did horns protrude? Or was all of this another trick of the shadows? Either way, Drouet knew she wouldn't have his company for long. She wished she had her doll again. She wanted to use its face as a mirror. She wanted to know that everything was still in place. But what Drouet had given away was now gone for good. She looked up, hoping for at least the comfort of a painted ceiling, another mural, but instead she saw the dome of an actual sky, dark and vast, full of twinkling red stars.

Swaingrove

Here, in the green glass light of the parlor, Swaingrove cultivates its memories. The house recalls the history of its own silent rooms, how they began as ideals, as uncreated forms. Long before the architects raised their beams and trusses, Swaingrove existed as an invisible body. It stood in the tall grass beneath tattered clouds and willow trees. Its flesh was a dream of paneled walls and wax wood floors. At times, it seemed to passersby that some vast and unknowable intelligence must have descended from the higher realms to crouch there on the hill. Animals avoided the grassy slope. Birds found other skies.

"Most houses gather dust," the aging Viscount d'Archambault told a handsome young soldier of the Confederacy, as the two of them sat together on the rose-colored divan in Swaingrove's grand parlor. "My house, dear boy, gathers *desires*."

The soldier, called Sam, had fine black hair, cropped short, a precaution against the recent infestation of lice in the barracks. His skin had the pale and sickly sheen of one who'd been too long in the winter regiments. He smelled of horse sweat and gunpowder. He kept his brass buttons polished. His leather boots, though worn, bore signs of good care. The viscount, a long-time friend of the regiment's commanding officer, Colonel Joseph, had made some pretense of cigars. He'd promised the boy a glass of strong brandy too if he came and sat for a time. But, in the end, there was neither cigar nor brandy. The house, in fact, seemed oddly bare.

The viscount reached out with his papery hand to touch the young soldier's downy-bearded cheek. The caress seemed to express something more than mere admiration. And because of this, the boy drew back, though only slightly. He didn't want to appear rude or foolish. He'd never been touched in such a manner before. There'd been no girls for him in the town he'd come from. No courting of any sort. He'd certainly not imagined a touch like that in the green light of Swaingrove's parlor. The viscount—white-haired and wearing an overlarge suit—smiled kindly enough. The noble air of the old man's French ancestry hung about him. He'd come to America some thirty years before. The gray waters of the Atlantic still colored his eyes. "They're sending children to war these days, aren't they?" the viscount said in a tone that might have well described his own shame at what the South had become. He allowed his fingers to trail down the breast of the young man's uniform, enjoying the firmness of a youthful chest. "When I was your age—" he said.

The solider gently took hold of the old man's wrist, attempting to stop the viscount's curious stroking. "Sir," the boy said. He had a faint accent. A pleasant hint of rural Georgia.

The viscount merely smiled again and removed his hand, as if the whole thing might have been some mistake.

"When I was your age," he said. "I would walk along the riverbank near my father's house. The water there was clear, like the mirror atop my mother's dresser. I could see myself reflected in that water. Just a boy, tripping along over rocks and stones."

"I knew a river once—" the young soldier began. He intended to tell a story of his own, as the soldiers did around the campfire. They spoke mainly of girls they'd left in their hometowns, but sometimes there were other stories too, those of high adventure, set along back roads and other unknown places. These were the landscapes that caused young men to feel the world had been made for them.

"Memories are like that, aren't they?" the viscount said, interrupting the soldier before he could even begin. "They trip along. Like a reflection over water. Always threatening to disappear." He slid his hand across the divan and let it rest in a place near the young man's strong thigh.

At that moment, the house shuddered around them, creaking its beams and momentarily causing the window glass to tremble. It was as if, the soldier thought, the whole of the structure had contracted like a muscle, pulling inward upon itself. A flicker, too fast for the eye to see. The soldier looked toward the green chandelier that swung now on its silver chain, casting odd shadows.

"You'll have to excuse Swaingrove," the viscount said. "My house is surely haunted."

The soldier raised his unblemished brow at this. He was no child on his mother's knee, to be sure, yet he'd heard tales from the other soldiers about this place. *The old man thinks he can conjure hexes . . . there's a painting in the hall . . . D'Archambault claims to have bought it off the back of a wagon driven by some wraith. And there's worse things too. . .* The young soldier hadn't seen any paintings, and he didn't believe spirits drove wagons around back-country roads. He'd agreed to visit Swaingrove because the promised glass of brandy sounded restorative. And the viscount hadn't seemed so terrible. He was a friend of the colonel, after all. What harm could such an old gentleman bring? "Haunted by whom, sir?" the soldier asked finally.

"Oh, ages of the dead, I suppose," the viscount replied. "People too often make the mistake of believing revenants are local in time. But ghosts tend to stay on, son. I imagine my haunts go back long before I laid the foundation of Swaingrove. There's probably more than a few red Indians crawling about. Right along with my house-girl who came to her end after falling down the stairs from the landing. And there's the man called Jonny who put a shotgun to his head in the cellar. There was the little baby too. Terrible thing. Sent my wife into paroxysms of grief. Our poor little child all laid out in white coffin lace." The viscount shook his head. "Now where were we?" he said.

"Colonel Joseph calls roll at nine o'clock, sir," the soldier said. "I should be going."

"Beauregard will understand," the viscount replied. "He is a merciful man."

But the young soldier persisted, standing from the divan and adjusting his uniform jacket. At this, some joint or brace deep inside the house began to squeal. It was an alarming sound, like a child in pain. And it seemed, for a moment, as if the whole house might suddenly collapse.

"Oh, you've done it now," the viscount said. And he looked as if he found something amusing.

"Done what?" the soldier asked.

The viscount stood and moved toward the boy again.

The soldier retreated to the lamplit foyer, reaching for the brass handle of the door.

"You'll find it locked, I'm afraid," the viscount said.

The soldier tried the handle and, indeed, the door was locked. For a moment, it seemed not even to be a door at all, but instead some kind of dry flesh that wanted his touch. "The key?" he said.

"Dark and lovely," the viscount replied, looking at the boy. "Dark and lovely."

At this, the soldier heard something on the stairs: the sound of a man or woman descending. Step after slow and measured step. The noise faltered once or twice, as if the person who descended (if it *was* a person at all) was injured or had some kind of ailment. The soldier watched for a shadow to appear, that of a servant perhaps or the viscount's wife. But when nothing came down from the rose-papered landing, he began to wonder if the stairs themselves might be making their own curious sounds. The footsteps were memories, old thoughts buried deep inside the wood.

The soldier paused then. For beyond the stairs, in the long dim foyer, there had appeared a large oil painting in a gilded frame. It was the sort of painting that might have been found in the halls of some grand museum, the likes of which the soldier knew he would never visit. He hadn't noticed the painting before, but now it seemed to be the most important thing in the entire house, a sprawling work, vast and detailed. And it appeared (yes, the soldier was quite sure this was true) the painting appeared to radiate with some light, as if a gas lamp glowed behind its canvas.

The scene, depicted in careful brushstrokes, was a sylvan glen where a group of fair young men reclined. Their limbs were long and languid. Their torsos shone in the sunlight. The soldier thought it might be a scene from history or perhaps a depiction of a tale from the viscount's home in France. A few of the young men in the painting wore scraps of peasant's clothes. Others wore almost nothing. All of them had a certain stillness in their handsome faces (*not like death*, the soldier thought, *but rather like a feeling of a great and final peace*). These men had not been to war. They had never known the handle of the plow. Or if they had once known those things, they had certainly forgotten.

Then it seemed as if their painted eyes—blue and green and silent black—had turned to gaze upon the young soldier in his ragged gray uniform. They appeared to wonder why the soldier had not yet joined them there in the beautiful sun.

"The house once told me—" the viscount said.

The rest of his words were lost, for a great rumbling came from beneath the two men as they stood in the foyer. It sounded as if a large object rolled through the root cellar, back and forth, making an awful noise.

"What did you say?" the soldier called. He was frightened now. He spoke loudly enough to be heard over the din. "What did the house tell you?"

"I call it Swaingrove for love, you know," the viscount replied, as if that was an answer to the soldier's question. "It didn't have a name before I gave it one."

The soldier felt as though he was about to have a nervous attack. The sharp report of rifle fire on the battlefield and the black thunder of mortar were nothing compared to Swaingrove. The house now shifted subtly and changed around him. The boy braced himself against the wall. He slid slowly down to the polished floor. The viscount knelt beside him, telling him it would be all right. "Things are different here at Swaingrove," the old man said. "But you mustn't worry, boy. And you mustn't leave me here all alone."

"I mustn't?" the soldier asked. It was hard to breathe. Difficult to even hold a thought.

"No," the viscount said. "You mustn't." He put his hand on the young man's forehead, as if checking for a fever. Then slowly he ran his fingers through the boy's short hair. "Every leave-taking is a kind of death. Don't you know that?"

The soldier didn't know if he should agree.

He closed his eyes. He imagined the bright grove in its gilded frame. He might rest there, he thought, away from the viscount, away from the house. Sunlight would fall between leafy branches. He'd lie among the figures, the elegant and peaceful men (nothing like corpses). And they would whisper their secrets to him.

The soldier felt the viscount unfastening the brass buttons of his gray uniform jacket. Swaingrove continued to shift around them. It certainly was a restless house. Perhaps it remembered how it had once crouched upon the hill, long before the viscount had come with his architects, long before the so-called ghosts had arisen. The house had been a deathless thing, a power to be reckoned with. And now? Well, now its uses were all too apparent.

"I was never your age, was I?" the viscount mused as he removed the soldier's shirt. He kissed the young man on his bearded cheek, then on his neck. "No, I was never your age at all."

Versailles, 1623

From the Private Reckonings of the King: On the morning of the hunt, the light was so thin my men carried torches. There, beyond the stables, I was granted a vision. The sky above Saint-Germain-en-Laye opened to me, and a marble hall appeared. A thousand candles burned among the clouds. And there was music too—the sort my father once bid his court musicians to play. I heard the sound of a harpsichord. A dreaming melody. I thought of my wife, still in our bed. During the night, she'd complained of spirits on the stairs. They woke her, she said, moving stealthily on bandaged feet. They were children, teeth bare and gleaming. They wore garlands of the sepulture. Their once bright lips and eyes were black and crusted with the brine of decay.

I did my best to soothe my wife. "There are no such children," I said.

"How do you know, my lord?" she asked.

"Because I am the king," I replied. "And I would not allow such a thing."

But on the morning of the hunt, I learned that I did not control the world. For I watched the sky reach down for me. A giant's finger pressed against a blue membrane. Something wanted to break through. A thing that lived there in the sky. My men had already released the hounds. The hawk made circles above. We were at the edge of the Woods of Marley. Shadows fell from the turning blades of a windmill on the hill. Sheets of silence moved. It was as if day and night were one.

I did not pursue the stag that morning. Nor did I use my longbow. Instead, the creature emerged from the woods of its own accord, its great rack of antlers the color of ivory. The stag knelt delicately before me. I used my sword to pierce its muscular throat. My blade sliced through its flesh. The color of the animal's pelt was the color of the palace I would build one day on that very spot: a pure and regal cream. And the blood of the stag was marble blue. When its throat was finally open, I saw a hall of mirrors shining there amongst the creature's precious bones. I remembered my father once saying, "Take heart—for I have conquered the world." I let him hold me then in his arms, and I wept at such a thought. I wondered if I too would one day be so strong.

"I will build a new palace," I told my wife when I returned from the Woods of Marley that day. "A glorious thing." My wife did not immediately respond. Perhaps she was still thinking of her dream, the children on the stair. "The gods," I said, "they've always hunted. But none, I think, has ever hunted as well as me." I was still covered in the stag's glorious blood. Covered in gold and mirrors. I didn't tell my wife about the sky. Or how it had reached for me. I didn't dare.

The Rite of Spring

Paddaburn Moor, 1919

After two weeks of rain, the river had risen to swallow an island of cattails near the dock. Reedy stems fluttered darkly in the stream. Elizabeth thought the morning sky, finally free of thunderheads, looked frail compared to the churning river. The water held a memory of the storm itself. From the dock, she watched the two boys in white shirts and ties prepare the rowboat—a flat-bottomed Whitehall owned by the school. By the look of its peeling paint and buckling hull, no amount of preparation could actually make the boat fit for water, but it would have to do. Headmaster Dove had insisted that a trip down the river, coupled with Elizabeth's fine interrogation skills, would dislodge the boys' secrets. "If anyone can get the truth from them it's you, Mrs. Jordan," Dove said, propped behind his desk, the lenses of his eyeglasses bright with the flare of a reflected sun. "You've become something of our little house detective, haven't you?"

Elizabeth wanted to respond tersely. She didn't approve of Dove's meandering, academic investigation. The proper authorities should have been called the moment the girl came out of the woods wearing only her undergarments. But Elizabeth restrained herself. Arguing with the headmaster was never productive. And an interview with the boys couldn't hurt. She did, in fact, trust her own methods of deduction.

※

On the boat dock, Elizabeth tucked one of her hands in the pocket of her overcoat for warmth. The other explored the ribs of her folded silk fan, an antique she'd pulled from the chest. Her mother had given the fan to her years ago, when she still thought of Elizabeth as the marrying kind. A good detective knew how to adopt the right character for an investigation, after all, and the boys, Conrad Deale and Martin Oole, might feel more at ease if they saw her not just as their stern Classics teacher, but also as a woman.

Her thoughts were disrupted when the larger of the two boys, Conrad Deale—the one she thought of as being in charge—turned from where he squatted boatside and said, "Maybe it's better if we don't take her out today, Mrs. J." His tone was calm. Unflustered by recent events. He leaned on one of the painted oars, as if it were a shepherd's staff. His body was mature-looking, though his face remained almost childlike.

"Why do you say that, Conrad?" Elizabeth asked, curling her fingers around her mother's fan. Conversation about the trip was unnecessary, but she would play along. Conrad Deale himself was aware that the outing was compulsory. They were going to the island to look at the purported scene of the crime.

Conrad loosened his school tie. "The river can get a little *difficult* when it's this high," he said, "especially around the other side of the hill there." He pointed to the grassy outcropping in the distance where Elizabeth sometimes sought out a comfortable place to read in the early months of summer after many of the boys had gone home. She found herself wishing that it was one of those warm days now, and that she was settled in the grass with a picnic of cheese and bread, reading passages from Ovid.

"We wouldn't want you to fall into the river, Mrs. J.," Conrad said. He grinned.

Elizabeth glanced at the other one, the foreigner, Martin Oole, to gauge his reaction to Conrad Deale's words. The thin blond boy worked away at his preparations, sweeping dead leaves from the bottom of the Whitehall into a bucket and dumping them into the water where they were then folded into darkness. Martin Oole's near fuguelike detachment had become a topic of conversation among teachers and staff alike at Harding. He'd been tested for various forms of deficiency and even retardation. The school nurses had come up with nothing.

"I have surprising skill when it comes to watercraft, I can assure you, Conrad," Elizabeth said, returning her attention to the more alert of the two boys. "I was on the rowing team as a girl."

Conrad Deale laughed. It was the sound of an entitled child who thought no trouble could come to him.

Elizabeth tapped the folded fan against her skirt impatiently.

"There's a mouse," Martin Oole said, poised in the boat with his bucket and broom. His voice was pitched higher than Conrad Deale's. Not pleasantly high like some of the other boys, but airy and goatish.

Conrad turned toward the boat. *"Alive,* Marty?"

Oole shook his head. "Dead. All shriveled. It doesn't have its eyes."

Elizabeth watched the two boys stare into the bottom of the Whitehall. "Don't be morbid," she said. "Just scrape the thing out and drop it into the water."

Conrad Deale turned toward her again as Oole pushed at the mouse with his boot. "No funerary rights, Mrs. J?" he said.

She drew her spine straight. "Mr. Deale, perhaps it's best if you play by the book today, considering your current situation."

Elizabeth watched as the body of the mouse fell head-first from the bucket into the river and was swallowed by the gulping currents. She couldn't help but think again of the poor farm girl who'd wandered out of the woods two nights before. The girl told a story about what Conrad Deale and Martin Oole had done to her and what they'd planned to do if she hadn't gotten away. Her name was June Strump—a sad name for a sad girl. The fact that the authorities had not yet been notified of her situation, that Headmaster Dove was keeping June at Harding School under the auspices of "examination and treatment" while he privately investigated the crime, was an injustice. The notion that June's own parents had been charmed by the headmaster and perhaps financially persuaded to leave her in his care, was most certainly obscene.

Conrad balanced himself in the center of the boat and helped Elizabeth into the stern. He instructed Martin Oole to take a seat in the prow, in case there were fallen branches that needed clearing. There'd been no doubt in Elizabeth's mind that Conrad would take it upon himself to row. His broad shoulders bespoke a *need* to row. The two boys faced Elizabeth, Oole's narrow visage peering from behind one of Conrad's shoulders, as if a vestigial head had sprouted there.

Martin Oole wound the rotted mooring rope as Conrad guided them onto the river that was not as choppy as it appeared from the dock. Elizabeth fluttered her fan and commented on the way the willow branches dipped into the stream and drew pictures in the water. All the while, she thought of June Strump, whom Headmaster Dove had allowed her to interview prior to this excursion. Looking at June had filled Elizabeth with an overwhelming sense of sympathy. There were bruises on the girl's doughy cheek where she said Conrad Deale had struck her. There were red scratches on her neck and chest as well from the boys dragging her by the legs through the underbrush. Her body was a map of their violence.

It was not precisely a confession that Elizabeth wanted from the boys on the boat. She already believed June Strump's story wholeheartedly. What she wanted instead was further information about the third figure in the woods that night, the man who June Strump claimed lurked behind the trees and watched as the boys beat and dragged her. The man whose existence the boys denied. If this adult watcher existed, he would change the entire nature of the event. He was the one Elizabeth wanted to incriminate.

"How are you both fairing in all this?" Elizabeth asked the boys. She hoped to draw them in, to appeal first to their emotions.

Conrad Deale dragged the oars through the water, guiding the boat past the tree-lined shores. "Tired mostly," he said. "The beds that Dove gave us are stuffed with straw. I don't see why we can't just sleep in our bunks. Why do we have to be separated out?"

"June Strump isn't sleeping well either, you know," Elizabeth said, happy to speak the girl's name to them. "Nor can she return to her own comfortable environs."

The boys were silent, which was to be expected, she supposed.

"June told me that if she sleeps," Elizabeth continued, "she has terrible dreams. Dreams about the woods. About the two of you—and the man who stood behind the trees."

This statement was followed only by the plash of the white oars in the water.

"Have you communicated with the man in the woods since your incarceration?" Elizabeth asked.

Conrad Deale raised the back of his hand to wipe sweat from his face. "I suppose we haven't, Mrs. Jordan," he said. "Since there *wasn't* any man. Like I told you already."

"And how about you, Martin?" Elizabeth asked. "You're being awfully quiet. Perhaps you've come down with one of your headaches."

Oole stared at her with bloodshot eyes. "I'm fine, Missus," he said softly. "I haven't got a headache."

"We only wanted to talk to her," Conrad Deale said, ceasing to row for a moment and allowing the boat to bob in the current. "In fact, *Marty* here wanted to talk to her. He thought she looked interesting when we saw her in the village. I disagreed. She looked cow-faced to me, but Marty hardly ever asks for anything so I let him invite her into the woods. We told her stories. Then everything got out of hand. The girl didn't understand what we were trying to say, just like I thought she wouldn't. She fought with us, tried to hurt us, and we fought back. We have bruises too, Mrs. J. Do you want to see them?"

"That's quite all right, Conrad," she said. Elizabeth had heard about the bruises and the scratches on the boys' chests and arms—like some animal had attacked them, the nurse had told her. Their clothing had been torn too when they came out of the woods. Elizabeth realized she'd been so preoccupied by her discussion with Conrad that she hadn't seen Martin was no longer engaged in their conversation. She adjusted her position in the boat so she could once again speak directly to him and saw he was staring off toward the left bank of the river. Not staring dreamily—as a boy who'd lost interest might—but staring with concentration at something on the far shore. She followed his gaze and saw nothing but sharp shadows of willow and birch trunks.

"What is it, Martin?" she asked. "What do you see out there?"

He seemed to have to force himself to look at her again. "I thought I saw an animal," he replied, voice hushed.

"Not another dead one, I hope?" she said.

"No, Missus," Oole said.

"Marty's got a good eye," Conrad said. "He's always seeing things I'd never catch."

"Is that why you've taken him as such a boon companion, Conrad?"

The boy shrugged. "We just fell in together. We talk."

"I'd like to hear about the subjects of your talks now," she said. "These so-called stories."

"We already told Headmaster Dove all of it," he countered.

She waved her now open fan, as if she needed air.

Conrad Deale lowered his chin, looking at her from beneath a furrowed brow. "You already know the kind of things we talk about, Mrs. J. You told us about them in the first place."

This quieted Elizabeth. She let the fan dip toward

the bottom of the boat. "What do you mean *I* told you?"

It wasn't Deale who responded. Instead, Martin Oole broke in, not directing his comment toward Elizabeth, but speaking instead to the wooded shore. "The Master of the Animals," he said.

Elizabeth recognized the name. She'd covered this figure as a topic in her class on antiquities, however briefly. It had been during a lecture on ancient cults. There were drawings of the Master of the Animals—or at least a figure very like him—on the walls of the caves at Lascaux. He was a creature dressed in skins, one who asked for human sacrifice in order to guarantee the fruitfulness of the hunt. Elizabeth's point of including such a figure in her lecture at all was to show the boys that religion was largely a function of circumstance. Gods were made as gods were needed. The Master of the Animals was really no more than a metaphysical gamekeeper imagined by men who wanted good luck in their endeavors. She devoted only a single class to such a topic because, though interesting for the boys, she found such things a bit too macabre. She didn't think the children needed their heads filled with notions of chthonic sacrifice and atavistic possession. She glared at Martin Oole and said bluntly, "Are you telling me that a story about a character from ancient mythology persuaded you to attempt to rape a farm girl?"

"We didn't do that, all right?" Conrad Deale interrupted. "We were trying to *demonstrate* something in the woods. She misinterpreted all of it."

Elizabeth sat back in the Whitehall, narrowing her gaze. "And what precisely were you trying to demonstrate?"

"We were performing a rite," he said. "A ritual. We had a hollowed out bull's horn that we found at the cigar shop in town. We filled it with wine—"

"Where did you get the wine?"

"We stole it from the cabinet in the kitchen," Conrad Deale said. "All the boys steal wine. June didn't like the horn though. She said she wasn't going to drink from something that an animal had grown on its head. So we moved to the next step."

"The next step," Elizabeth said. She attempted to control her anger. These were still only schoolboys. They were, perhaps, confused. "Did the man who stood behind the trees tell you to do these things?" she said.

"There was no man," Conrad repeated.

Elizabeth breathed deeply. "Tell me what happened next."

"We danced," he said.

"June liked the dancing," Martin Oole added. "But only for a while."

"She liked it until you forced her to take off her dress?" Elizabeth said.

"We didn't force her, Mrs. Jordan. She took off her clothes on her own." Conrad stopped here and looked uncharacteristically at a loss for words. Martin Oole appeared to grow agitated, and Elizabeth had the sudden thought that the young Frenchman was touching Conrad Deale's lower back, so she couldn't see, but so that Conrad would know to stop talking. It was in that silence that she heard a sound on the shore, the crack of a branch coupled with a rustle of trees.

"Gentlemen," Elizabeth said, "is there someone following alongside our boat right now?"

Both boys merely stared at her. In that moment, they were truly nothing more than children, frightened and wide-eyed. They were coming quite close, she could tell, to looking to her for guidance—she who'd told them the ridiculous story of the Master of the Animals. She who'd taught them about the rituals of sacrifice. Elizabeth wanted to reach out her hand to them, to simply ask them to come back and be good boys again. But in the next moment, Martin Oole spoke, breaking their moment of innocence. "I think it's a dog," he said. "But I can't tell."

"Why don't we ferry our boat over there where the sound came from and see what we can see," Elizabeth said.

"No," Oole said, and Conrad Deale craned his neck to look at his friend, once again ceasing to paddle and allowing them to drift in the center of the dark river. "I'm afraid of dogs," Oole said.

"Don't be ridiculous, Martin," Elizabeth said. "Conrad, if you would just maneuver us toward the far shore so we can get a better look at what's tracking us. Do as I say."

"Are you sure, Mrs. J.?" Conrad said.

"Of course I'm sure. I never speak unless I'm sure."

The boy worked the oars expertly, keeping the left one still and paddling with the right until the boat headed toward the far shore where the foliage was so thick that Elizabeth could not be sure if someone stood there watching them. If it was the third man that June Strump had talked about—the man who stood and watched from behind the trees—she wanted to see him for herself. Elizabeth wasn't afraid. She wouldn't allow herself that emotion. She was doing this for June, for the way the poor dear looked, sitting in the nurse's room, pretending to read the dry tomes that Headmaster Dove had left with her. Books that Elizabeth was fairly certain June couldn't understand. And why should she want to understand them—they were the instruments of the society that she'd fallen prey to.

Elizabeth tried hard not to see the trees themselves,

but rather to look between the branches at the narrow patches of dark and light for any shifting movement. But as the bow of the boat touched the reedy shore, Elizabeth was still not sure if there was anything to be seen at all.

※

Elizabeth said it might be better if they got some exercise. Sitting in the boat too long was making them all sluggish. This was, of course, a calculation intended to push the boys further beyond their own boundaries, to bring them closer to revealing the truth by taking them to the site itself. Elizabeth and the boys made the upward climb from the river, and she was glad she'd worn her boots with a shorter heel. Conrad Deale walked ahead and Martin Oole followed behind, muttering something under his breath in French. She was about to ask Oole what he was talking about when Conrad said, "What's that?" There was a significant amount of tension in his voice, especially for one normally so self-possessed. Elizabeth momentarily forgot about Martin Oole's mutterings. She focused on her progress through the trees to the place where Conrad Deale stood pointing at the ground. She gazed into the tangle of plant life at his feet, trying to see what he was so intrigued by.

"What do you mean, Conrad?" she said. "I don't see anything at all."

Conrad Deale hunched, staring at the empty patch of ground for a few more moments, then turned to her. "I guess it isn't anything," he said. "I was imagining things."

"What did you think you saw exactly?"

"Oh, it wasn't anything really, Mrs. J.," he said.

Elizabeth suddenly realized that Martin Oole no longer stood behind them. In fact, he'd disappeared entirely.

Conrad Deale's exclamations had provided camouflage for the boy's escape.

"Conrad, where is Martin?"

Conrad Deale leaned on the white oar that he'd carried with them from the boat. He appeared to consider her question and then said, "I suppose he's gone back to the river to drown himself, Mrs. Jordan."

At first, Elizabeth thought the boy was making a joke in bad taste, but when he did not laugh and continued to simply stand and stare at her, she asked, "Why would he want do that?"

Conrad Deale brushed perspiration from his upper lip with the back of his hand. "Because Marty's weak. He can't handle these sorts of things. He couldn't really handle the thing with the cow-faced girl either. That's why everything got out of control, if you have to know. Marty panicked. So the girl panicked. I think it's something in his French blood."

Elizabeth's heart beat so hard beneath her dark blouse that she thought it might cause the locket that hung against her breast to tremble. "What sort of thing are you talking about, Conrad? What can't Martin cope with?"

"The thing I have to do to you today," he replied, calmly.

She was not sure if she should turn and attempt to go back to the boat or simply flee into the woods. What Conrad Deale had said frightened her terribly. She wanted to leave, but the boy was certainly faster than she was. Any attempt at escape would be futile. Her only recourse at this point would be to reason with him. "I'm afraid I don't understand, Conrad," she said. "What do you mean that you *have* to do this thing?"

The boy raised his fine eyebrows, "I'm under orders,

Mrs. Jordan," he said.

Elizabeth's mind raced, trying to think of a way to lead the boy away from his intentions, but before she could speak, he said, "Do you really think some old story made us do what we did in the woods that night? You think we'd believe in such nonsense?"

"I—"

"That sort of fantasy is for bored old women, Mrs. J.," Conrad said. He took a step toward her, dragging the white oar behind him. "All that reading. All that stupid, useless talk. Us boys know better than to care about such things. The closest you can come to gods these days are men like Headmaster Dove. Men who can help us with our futures if we behave. We took the girl into the woods because the headmaster told us to. Dove wanted to watch. We're like *gods* to him—young and strong. We can do the things he can't. And we took you onto the river today because he told us to. Because he said that you're the only one who ever questions him. You don't listen. That's what he told us, Mrs. J."

"Conrad, you can't expect me to believe that a civilized man like Headmaster Dove sent me out here to be harmed by my students," she said.

The boy took another step toward her. At the same time, he raised the white oar. "Not harmed, Mrs. J.," he said. "Sacrificed."

Elizabeth lifted her hands, one of which still clung to the pitiful silk fan from her mother. She knew that such an attempt to block Conrad Deale's blow was useless. He could easily knock her to the ground. For a moment, she seemed to drift in the air above her own body. She saw herself cowering like an animal before him. And just as the white oar swung toward her face, a loud knock echoed against the trees, sharp enough to make it seem as though a ripple had moved through the landscape itself.

The oar didn't strike Elizabeth. Instead, Conrad Deale dropped it from his hands.

Deale stood before her, blood boiling from a cut that had opened on his high white forehead. A red stream of the stuff ran down his face and neck. Elizabeth saw a large stone lying at Deale's feet. The stone still had a piece of his skin clinging to its sharp edge. Conrad Deale's knees buckled suddenly. He toppled forward, landing face down in the mud.

Martin Oole stumbled out of the trees. He held a second stone of approximately the same size as the one that had struck Conrad Deale. He made a strange high-pitched squeal that turned into something like a scream. The French boy had saved her. And in doing so, something had broken loose inside him. Elizabeth went to him, intending to provide comfort, but before she could reach him, Martin Oole's hand—the one holding the second stone—shot up, smashing the rock into his own face. He repeated this action three times before Elizabeth could reach him, bursting his nose open like a boil and breaking off both of his front teeth. She grabbed his arms and shook him, forcing the bloodied rock to drop from his fingers. "Stop it, Martin," she yelled. "Stop it right now."

Oole only stared at her. His face was a red mask. He didn't seem to know her. He didn't seem to know anything. Finally he whispered, "You have to go now. He's coming."

"Are you talking about Headmaster Dove?" Elizabeth said, looking about.

The boy shook his head. "The *other* master."

She started to tell Martin Oole that everything would be fine, that she could take him to a doctor in town. The doctor would tend his wounds. Then they would get him safely back to his parents. But just as she began to speak, a noise rose from depths of the forest—an awful trumpeting, like the call of an ancient horn. It was the kind of sound that made the trees shudder and the river hush.

Elizabeth looked into Martin Oole's bloodied face once more. She put her hands on his shoulders. "Who is coming?" she whispered. "Tell me the truth, Martin."

"Conrad talked to Headmaster Dove," Martin replied. "But *I* talked to the other one. I've always talked to the other one, Missus."

Elizabeth heard something approaching now. It sounded as if it was running. Loping through the forest. She thought of June Strump locked away in the school by Headmaster Dove. She thought of how the boys had hurt June that night on Dove's orders—because he wanted to watch. She pictured the horrors enacted in the woods that night. She wondered what sort of being such actions might have conjured.

Elizabeth suddenly wanted to close her hands around Martin Oole's slender throat. She wanted to put an end to all of this.

But instead she whispered, "Go, Martin. Leave this place."

The boy ran off into the woods, crashing through the trees.

Elizabeth turned then very slowly. She thought of all the lessons she'd taught the boys, all the ancient mysteries she'd piled upon them. She pictured the horned figure painted on the caves at Lascaux. She pictured the boys' upturned, listening faces. There was a difference, she thought, between a god and monster. She should have told them while she could.

Homunculus

Salzburg, 1535

Paracelsus, the great alchemist, is asleep in the alcove when the homunculus finally emerges from its gourd-shaped glass. Imagine the creature: a tiny, blood-filled form. Its mouth is no bigger than a nail's head. Its teeth are like granules of sugar. It stands at the edge of the workbench, flushed and silent, peering warily into the chalky recesses of the master's room. Above the fireplace hangs an accordion bellows, a dark and portentous wing. Iron troughs and copper tubes form a complex city beneath a plaster sky. Snow crusted on the windowsill throws spangled light across the wall. The near translucent homunculus lifts its sliver of a hand, and for a moment, the hand is gloved in light. The creature feels warmth. It hears its master stirring.

Upon awakening, Paracelsus sees the homunculus on the workbench, and he rises, gathering a sheet around his aging body. He is startled by the results of his experiment—this shrunken and skinless child. He has never taken a wife. There were men in Germany and then again in the African mines, but nothing remains of those friendships. The alchemist never expected a family, and he wonders if he should dare to call the unlikely thing that stares back at him a son.

We have only the old physician's fragmentary notes to reconstruct this meeting. "The homunculus has many features of a child that is born from a woman," he writes, "but it would be wrong to mistake it for that. The creature comes from me alone. And because of this, it is mine to care for. As I hold it in my arms, it has the strange air of one who sees the invisible wheels of Heaven. Forty days in the glass cucurbit were enough to give my seed time to agitate. This same number of days was required for Egyptian embalmment. It was forty as well for Christ's awakening in the wilderness. Forty more after the Resurrection when He rose again. The birth of the homunculus is admittedly a mystical occurrence—one that I do not think my scientific mind will ever fully comprehend."

In his journal, Paracelsus makes a record of the creature's care. A homunculus must be nourished, he tells us. Human blood is ideal. It fattens and rouges the delicate body. The old man cuts his finger daily and allows the creature to sip the red bead that forms at the base of the incision. The homunculus must be educated as well, though not with books or dictation. The education of a homunculus is best performed in the natural world. If correctly taught, it is foretold by both Ficino and Agrippa that the creature will become a master of nature itself, one who can raise armies of bizarre forms: giants and wood-sprites, worricows and naiads. "Those beings who understand the hidden matters of the Earth," Paracelsus writes.

Picture the alchemist tramping through a dark forest at the base of the Swiss Alps. He holds his homunculus gingerly in the crook of his arm. The creature's pink legs dangle like those of a child. "Chestnut tree," the old man says, pointing. "And here—a puddle of rain water." The water seems to swell and contract as the homunculus observes it. The chestnut tree too looks as if it might burst open and give birth to mysteries that have been long dreaming within. When the old alchemist coughs, the creature turns its small head to look at him, gazing out from beneath heavy pink lids. Paracelsus attempts a smile, revealing stained teeth. "Old man," Paracelsus says, touching his own hollow breast. "Terrible weak old thing."

Paracelsus writes that when not being educated, the homunculus is stored in a cupboard or concealed in some other even darker place. He tells us that he has begun to realize the uneducated homunculus is like an unpolished mirror, the surface of which is distorting but somehow all the more revealing because of its imperfection. "How many of us have caught glimpses of ourselves in a poor surface of reflection and been taken aback by our own terrible nature? A badly made mirror may not reveal the precise lines of the face, but it can instead show the very essence of a soul. To look at the homunculus, therefore, is to see oneself aslant. The homunculus provides a truer vision."

The alchemist's journal is rife with descriptions of evenings spent by the fire, listening to the creature move about in its locked cabinet. "The homunculus sounds neither frightened nor displeased," Paracelsus writes. "It merely paces, as I sometimes pace when I am deep in thought. Perhaps, there in the dark, it considers its lessons. Or more likely still, it concerns itself with subjects beyond my own reckoning."

At times, the alchemist seems to grow weary of considering the homunculus's secret knowledge. He digresses, writing of his mother in Einsiedeln. She died when he was very young. He placed small red flowers on her grave—

Dianthus, gathered from her own garden. The memory of those blossoms reminds him of the homunculus's own delicate face. "When I hold the creature, it is as though one of mother's red funeral flowers is staring up at me," he writes. "I can almost see the gentle curve of the petals and smell the sweetness of those long ago days."

Paracelsus recalls the priests who taught him the sciences at the stone abbey in Carinthia. He makes a list of their names. Father Brandt was particularly kind, teaching him the specifics of botany and metallurgy. The alchemist wonders what the priest would make of the homunculus locked away in the cabinet. Would he perceive it as a product of science or some ethereal body, unwisely gathered from the upper air? Paracelsus goes on to tell us of his journeys in Africa where he worked in the mines, searching for precious metals that could be used in his experiments. He treasured being alone with the men in the darkness, listening to their stories. He remembers coming up out of the throat of the Earth, hands and face caked in soot. He had to close his eyes against the bright light of the African day.

Finally, Paracelsus writes: "How should we imagine the light will look on the morning when the homunculus stirs in its cupboard, ready for release, but I myself do not awake? Certainly, that day is coming. I can feel the weight of it in my chest. Will it be the salt-colored light of my own dreams that fills the workroom? Or will it be the dim, gray light of abandonment? How long will the tiny body knock against the cabinet door? Will the homunculus eventually find a voice to call for me? I imagine the pitiful sound spreading into the workroom and then to the city beyond, growing thinner, leaving only a few strangers in the street unsure if they've heard anything at all."

The Coil

Arthur awakes in the golden wood. He has dreamed of a silver cup or a stone that fell from the sky. He cannot remember which and wonders if such things can be said to matter any longer. The campfire has gone out. His bedroll is covered in morning dew. He watches mistletoe flutter on the branch of a tall birch and listens to the bright song of a jay. The journey, he realizes, is ending. Two weeks out, and nearly done. The forest seems as if it might close around him like a giant eye. Soon there will only be the remembrance of these travels. Half-invented tales told to other men in a shadowed hall. Arthur stands and makes his way toward the stream near the encampment, careful not to wake Sir Guyon. The knight looks handsome there in his bedroll—tangle of yellow hair, bristle of a young man's beard. Arthur remembers how the two of them used to play together in the barley fields west of the castle—Fox and Goose and Hoodman's Blind.

Arthur kneels before the stream. Shadows glide across the surface of the water. He knows what must happen next if the quest is to continue (and it must continue. Arthur won't go back . . . not yet). He's learned his occult imagination from the most convincing of prophets.

He relaxes his gaze. Blurs his vision. And there, twisting in the ripples of the water, he sees it: a kind of answer. "What have you found, my lord?" Sir Guyon asks, approaching from behind, eyes still bleary with sleep. He wears only his breeches and a coarse linen shirt. Arthur pauses for a moment and then holds his hand out over the water. Guyon looks down and sees nothing. Of course he doesn't. There's nothing to be seen. "Darkness," Arthur says, gravely. "And a presage."

"Of what?" Guyon asks.

Arthur peers at the water, as if it's become a scryer's stone. "Cruelly scaled and long-bodied," he says. "A devil, of sorts."

Sir Guyon takes a step back from the water, and Arthur is pleased. It's always fear first with the knights, then bravery. He wonders for a moment if Guyon has ever been in love. The knight has pretended at such emotion, of course. All of them do. They write letters to maidens in a thick and unschooled hand. But has he ever felt what Arthur feels now—the cruel sting of it?

The two of them ready themselves. The serpent, Arthur says, is hidden in a cave on the mountain pass above. Guyon bows his head in prayer, lips moving. He speaks to God as only a young man can. Arthur prays too, but not about a dragon. They gather the bedrolls then and begin their travels, Guyon in the lead. Arthur carefully watches the knight's strong neck, the movement of his lean shoulders. He wonders if a quest like this could be made to last forever. Time might swallow them. Their names would appear side by side in ages of poetry. Their souls would mix forever in the higher air.

When they reach the cave—for there actually is a cave on the mountain pass, much to Arthur's surprise—

Guyon draws his broadsword. "Does it sleep, my lord?" Guyon asks.

Dragons are made of sleep, Arthur thinks. For they themselves are dreams. "Sir Guyon," he says, and the knight turns to look at him, clear-eyed and fine. There are too many words behind Arthur's teeth. None of them will come out.

Guyon raises his brow. "What is it, my lord?" he asks.

Arthur shakes his head. "Tread carefully, noble friend."

And together they move into the darkness of the cave. Guyon lights a torch, but the flame is dim and only serves to make more shadows. They progress down a narrow passage, and Arthur is reminded of the musty tombs beneath the castle. This place too smells of death.

"I can hear the monster breathing," Guyon whispers.

Arthur does not want to believe this. He invented the creature after all. In fact, he's invented all the fabulous things that populate their quests. None of them are real. There is no vast Green Knight. No ghost-white stag. Such things are extensions of his passion. Emotion manifest. Another reason to drag Sir Guyon into the woods.

And yet he too can hear something now, a ragged sound that echoes against the cave walls. The smell of death mixes with the scent of smoke. Guyon slips on loose stone, and Arthur watches as his friend tumbles into a large, shallow chamber.

"Here," Guyon hisses, righting himself. "Look, my lord."

But Arthur doesn't need to look. He can feel it. Something has gone wrong. Sir Guyon is advancing on a scaled coil at the center of the stone chamber, excited because, after all this time, he has finally found something to slay. "Wait," Arthur says, but the coil is already unknotting itself there in the dark. Arthur sees a serpent's head. The creature's eyes are nothing like love. They are white. They are blank stones. Like years of waiting. Like terrible yearning. And Arthur wonders what he might do to make this right. Is there a way to kill the thing in his heart before it does what it intends to do?

Sleep and Death

1.

Pascal shifted inside the ornate vestibule of the Musée de Vieux. Stone angels with mouths agape stared down at him from a high, encrusted ceiling. A smell of dust and moldering canvases pervaded. He peered through the thick, wavy glass of a leaded windowpane at the museum's courtyard beyond. Rain trembled the white chrysanthemums in the small garden. Carriages creaked through rutted mud. His aunt, ancient and wary as she was, had warned him against venturing out that morning. "There's a storm on its way," she said. "A fearsome one. I saw a large blackbird. I heard a distant chime." Pascal was not afraid of the rain, and he did not believe in portents. He was nineteen and had his strength about him. Today, however, he wore a new gray suit. His cousin Elise had sent it from Montparnasse. He did not want to sully the suit's beautiful silk. So instead of walking in the rain, he decided he would linger at the museum for a time. An old woman, a docent, pressed a printed map into his hand. Pascal took the map and nodded. He didn't intend to look at art. There would be more interesting exhibits at the Musée de Vieux that day.

It had become Pascal's habit, in every public space, to watch men. Young men or old, it did not matter. As long as they were handsome. As long as he could dream about them. He disregarded everything else. Decorations were exhausting. Women, of no interest. He liked men who were tall, men who had brooding faccs. He often imagined what a man's lips would taste like (cigar smoke or the blood of red meat). He wondered what it would feel like to kiss the delicate hair on a man's chest. Or to put his hands around a man's smooth waist and draw him close. Pascal's imagination had grown so powerful, so intoxicating, that he could become intimate with any stranger he encountered without even as much as saying hello. He made love to phantoms in the aisles of the marketplace and on the soot-spoiled platforms of the train station. He drank the sweat from ghosts. His aunt had once glared at him with her single good eye and said: "Pascal, your mother always feared you might go—how should I say—Greek." He'd concealed a grimace. No one should ever know of his desires. To be discovered would be a kind of death. "I'm Frcnch, my dear," he assured her, patting his aunt's liver-spotted hand and maintaining his composure. "As French as you or poor dead Mama."

In one gray corner of the museum, Pascal found what he was looking for: a young man standing before a painting. He was blond-haired, beardless. His wide shoulders impressively filled out his traveling suit. And he held himself with a certain sense of fortitude, as one who had perhaps taken part in various rugged sports at school. The painting that captured his interest depicted two dark haired youths. They lay, entwined, on a low velvet couch. The lither of the two held a bouquet of red poppies, and he rested his head on the broader youth's shoulder. Both appeared as if they might never stir again. Behind their sofa, a colonnade opened onto a star-filled night.

Pascal observed the painting in silence, edging as close to the blond young man as he dared. He imagined removing the man's suit jacket, unbuttoning his linen shirt. He would rub his lips against the young man's shoulders. He would slide his tongue along his ruddy neck.

Then, something surprising.

The object of Pascal's unfolding fantasy turned. "What do you think of it?" the young man said.

Pascal only stared at him for a moment. Such a thing as this had never happened before. And he wondered briefly if he'd imagined the words.

"I'm sorry," the young man said, running one hand through his thick blond hair. "I don't speak much French."

"American?" Pascal asked, feeling a pleasurable chill.

The young man gave a nod. "Nobody here speaks English. It's not like Paris."

"My mother, she—" Pascal said, pausing to search for the word. "She instructed me."

The young American grinned. Such a handsome grin. "What a lovely mother," he said. "So these two—" He pointed at the silent youths in the painting. "What do you think?"

"They are—" Pascal said, looking at the still bodies once more. It suddenly occurred to him that they might be corpses. They were so pale. So calm. He knew this was absurd. But he could not stop himself from saying: "Are they dead?"

"Oh no," the young man said. "No, no. They're gods. Lesser gods. One is Sleep. The other is Death. Brothers."

Pascal rubbed a finger against his chin, examining the painting further. "They look—not like brothers."

The American laughed. "Alexander Hartford," he said, extending his hand. Pascal shook it and introduced himself. "All the gods are brothers," Alexander continued. "But these two in particular—these two—I'm going to use them in my argument."

"Argument?" Pascal asked.

"A paper," Alexander said. "For my dissertation."

"You are a student?" Pascal said.

"That's right."

Pascal allowed himself to drift once more into fantasy. As a boy, he'd read many romantic novels. The idea of an American student traveling alone in France made him feel positively lightheaded. He wished his life might ever be so exciting. "Sleep and Death," Pascal repeated, looking at the painting. He enjoyed the way Alexander smelled—like the dark American wilderness.

Alexander cleared his throat, looking back at the painting. He appeared to consider something before speaking. "Which do you imagine yourself to be?" he asked finally. "Sleep or Death?"

"Which?" Pascal asked, surprised by the question. For what could such a question mean? "They're very much alike, aren't they?"

"You must be Sleep then," Alexander said, taking a step closer. "Sleep is unsure. Death always knows his purpose."

Pascal ran his fingers through his own dark hair, feeling the dampness of it. He wondered what might be happening. He was suddenly afraid to imagine anything beyond this moment.

Alexander smiled. "Maybe we should go down the

street, " he said. "The little cups of coffee that they serve at the shop on the corner—they look, well, just right."

2.

At the coffee house, seated before a large window, Alexander talked about his paper as he sipped coffee from a bone-colored cup. Most of what he said, Pascal did not understand (something about the effect of religious art on the human mind . . . the significance of the icon.) Yet when Alexander stopped speaking, Pascal said he approved of the ideas. He felt so nervous. He wasn't sure what else he *could* say.

"I think you might be the sort who likes almost everything, aren't you?" Alexander said.

"Today," Pascal replied, feeling a blush rise on his cheeks. "Today, I suppose I am."

"Do you want to know more?" Alexander asked. "Would you like to accompany me on my investigations tomorrow? I could use an assistant."

"Please," Pascal said, having wanted nothing more in his entire life. "Please, yes I would."

3.

They met for a light breakfast the next morning. Alexander announced they would go to the ruin of a church at the western edge of the city where they would observe a number of frescoes. By the time this decision was made, a giddy fresh feeling had come over Pascal, the sort of emotion that triumphs over dust. His aunt had watched him leave the house that morning. She'd been seated in her high-backed wooden chair. She looked like the Queen of the Dead, he thought, arrayed on a ghastly throne. "And where are you going today, my dear?" she'd intoned.

"To see someone," he replied. "A friend."

"You have no friends here, Pascal," she said. "You have only just arrived in Nîmes."

"I've been here six months," he said. "I met him yesterday."

She stared at her nephew. "You must be careful about *new* friends," she replied. "I have always kept to old friends myself. The "new" is often remarkably dangerous."

Pascal and Alexander made their way down the narrow, cobbled streets, laughing together. The persistent antiquities of Nîmes seemed to flower in their presence.

"*New* friends," Alexander said, laughing after Pascal had told him the story. "They are the very best sort, I should think."

"My aunt thinks I should stay always at home," Pascal replied. "She thinks I should mourn my mother's passing."

"Your mother?" Alexander asked, looking surprised. "She is dead?"

"It's been half a year."

"I'm sorry. I didn't—"

"We don't need to talk about it now," Pascal said.

"No?" Alexander said.

"No," Pascal replied. He brushed the young American's hand with his own and then walked on.

4.

Later that evening, Pascal found himself drunk on wine. He and Alexander sat together in a candlelit café. Alexander seemed even more emboldened than usual. Every word that sprang from him seemed of a new and vibrant tongue.

"Do you know the story of Apollo and his male friend Hyacinthus?" Alexander asked.

Pascal raised his brow. "I suppose I do." A youth and a god, he thought. They fell in love. One of them became a flower.

"What about Achilles and Patroclus?"

"Of course."

"And do you believe in—as they say—beloved friendship? Between men, that is."

Pascal smiled faintly. "There are so many stories. How can it not be true?"

They both paused. They sipped their wine.

"What if two men should find themselves in such a state?" Alexander asked finally. "What should they do?"

Pascal pondered this, staring into his glass of dark wine. He thought of his aunt. He thought of his mother. "They could both drink poison, I suppose. Put themselves out of their misery."

"I don't think so," Alexander said.

"Or they could flaunt convention? Do as they please."

Alexander leaned back in his chair, lacing his fingers behind his head. "There we are." He reached forward suddenly and touched Pascal's hand. "You're such a surprise, you know that?" he said.

Pascal took another sip of wine. "So are you."

5.

In the days that followed, the world around the two men shimmered with fantasy. Pascal spent his nights dreaming a life with Alexander. Perhaps they would live together in the countryside: tend a small farm, read poetry, make music. For the rest of their days, they'd exist in a kind of bliss among sheep and goats. He liked picturing Alexander in rough peasant's garments, carrying wood.

After supper one night, Pascal's aunt spoke to him from the shadows of her velvet drawing room. "And how is your *new* friend, my dear?"

"He is well," Pascal said. "He is an American."

"Christ's blood," his aunt said. "What foolish game are you on about?"

"It's good to know someone," Pascal said. "This city has been a lonely place."

"The Americans are nothing but rudeness and vigor. You'll certainly collapse if you attempt to follow him about."

"I doubt that," Pascal said.

"Your mother is *dead*."

"She is," he replied. "But I have recently discovered that I am not."

6.

Pascal and Alexander visited an old chapel one evening to see another relic. A local priest had forbidden them to enter the place, but they'd gone anyway when the priest had ventured off for his dinner. Alexander said that, even if the old man returned, he'd be drunk, and they could easily escape him. Disobedience, Pascal had begun to realize, was part of the fun in Nîmes. Everyone moved so slowly in the old city. One could never be caught for anything.

The tapestry they aimed to see hung behind a wooden partition and was illuminated only by the light of the boys' own lantern. "The greatest of the sacred arts," Alexander said, "makes the invisible world visible." He touched Pascal's arm as the two of them stood before the vast and threadbare tapestry. The scene displayed was a Greek pastoral—playful erotics in a sunlit field.

Young men and women lay together in various states of undress. Over the years, this particular field had grown gloom-ridden. Gray nymphs and yellowed satyrs could be seen lurking in the surrounding woods.

In one corner of the tapestry, rising from the woolen grass, was a pale figure. The figure didn't immediately draw Pascal's attention. The bodies in springtime ecstasy were more obviously compelling. But then slowly, Pascal's gaze gravitated toward that lonely figure. The creature, he thought, was difficult to see even when Alexander held the lamp close, and the yellow light spilled out over the woven surface. The figure stood on two legs, and its body was covered in a layer of dirty white hair. No elegant horns sprouted from its head, nor did it carry any antique musical instrument. It was a blunt form, simian in appearance. A sort of pale ape, though not precisely an ape. It had terrible eyes. Pascal later thought they were not like eyes at all. They were instead bleak instruments, orifices that did not gather images but devoured them. The white ape appeared to study the lovers in the field.

"What god is that?" Pascal asked, not wanting to get any closer to the pale form. He hoped there would be some explanation, just as there had been with the figures of Sleep and Death.

Alexander knelt before the image to get a better look. "I don't—" he said. "It looks like it was added. It doesn't belong."

"Who would put such a thing there?" Pascal said, gazing at the beast.

Alexander shook his head.

"We could ask the old priest," Pascal said.

"He wouldn't know," Alexander said, glancing again at the tapestry. "And even if he did, I don't think he'd tell us."

As they spoke, Pascal felt as though the creature's regard had suddenly and impossibly fallen upon the two of them. It was as if the beast—covered in its blight of hair—had heard them speaking quietly in the nave. And now it watched the two boys as it had previously watched the lovers in the field. This presented a sort of upset in Pascal's heart. The fantasy he'd been living for the last few weeks with Alexander suddenly seemed under great and inescapable scrutiny.

Alexander must have felt the beast's gaze as well because he bowed his head, as one might in the presence of something holy.

"It's come to haunt them," Pascal said. "To haunt the people in the field. It wants to make them miserable."

Alexander remained silent.

It was in that moment that the young American appeared transformed. His face—the face Pascal had come to think of as the most beautiful he'd ever seen—appeared glasslike, fragile. The light of the lantern actually seemed to pass through Alexander's flesh. All the futures Pascal had dreamed for them became as thin and fragile as that face.

"The priest was right," Alexander said. "We shouldn't be here."

"They should take the thing down," Pascal replied. "Put it in a chest."

7.

Pascal and Alexander left the chapel just as the stars were beginning to shine. That evening, they got drunk on tavern wine again. But the wine tasted sour, and Pascal felt sick from it. Together, they stumbled back to Alexander's rented rooms and ended up in the same bed, entwined like Sleep and Death. It didn't feel like they were gods though. It felt like something altogether different.

Pascal awoke that night, startled. He felt a presence at the foot of Alexander's bed. He couldn't quite see the figure, but he could *feel* it watching them. And he could smell it too. A scent like ashes. Like old death. Pascal imagined that the tall shadow at the end of the bed was the creature from the tapestry. Something ancient and watchful. Something that stood beyond the ages of man. It didn't care for the two boys. It didn't care for anyone. It hailed from a silent realm. A place where things were meant to remain invisible. Pascal called out, loudly enough to awake Alexander.

"What do you mean, the creature was here?" Alexander asked after Pascal explained what he'd seen, half in English, half in French.

"It followed us," Pascal said. "It *sees* us."

Alexander rolled away, facing the wall. "Go to sleep, Pascal," he said. "You're drunk."

8.

The two boys saw less of each other after that. Alexander announced that he would soon be leaving Nîmes. He'd come across a description of a church in London with paintings of Paradise. He said he needed to view it for his project.

"Isn't this paradise enough?" Pascal asked. It was an attempt at humor. Yet he found he felt disgusted by the desperate sound of his own voice.

Alexander looked away, pretending to be distracted by a white chicken roaming the cobbled street.

9.

"And where is your new friend?" Pascal's aunt asked one evening when she saw him seated alone in the library of the dark house. The rasp of her voice was almost too much for him. She was like some gray revenant in the doorway.

"He's gone," Pascal said.

His aunt swayed in the threshold, squeezing the black handle of her walking stick. "Back to America?" she asked.

"No," Pascal replied flatly. "Just gone away."

"These things happen, my dear." There was a note of sympathy.

"Yes," Pascal replied. "For the rest of my life, I suppose."

10.

Pascal's cousin, Elise, came to visit Nîmes in the month that followed. She was a pretty, dark-haired girl with ambitions of marriage. She was also the sort of person Pascal could sometimes reveal things to. Elise had a way of not being shocked—largely due to her own self-involvement. They sat together at an outdoor café, and Pascal told his cousin about his time with Alexander.

"The world of men," Elise said before Pascal had finished. "I cannot say I understand it. What did auntie say?"

"She was afraid," Pascal said. "And then I was afraid. I wonder if I'll ever be free of him—the memory, I mean."

Elise adjusted the satin folds of her dress. Wordlessly, she peered down the boulevard, as if the cold wind there had suddenly cohered and become a visible body. Pascal wondered, for a moment, if his cousin really could see something there. The thought frightened him all the more.

Elise began talking of her own mother's interest in planning a wedding. "She wants *white lilies*, of all things, near the altar," Elise said. "Can you imagine that, Pascal?"

"Like a funeral," he said.

Elise shook her head. "The very same."

Night Is Nearly Done

1.

When no bear was in the fighting ring, the metal collar lay in the dust—a black shackle, shot with rivets, fitted with an adjustable hinge. The Bear Master invited patrons to examine the collar before the fight, and men like my father spent time listening to the satisfying snick of the latch and discussing the finer points of its construction. Father threatened to put the thing around my own neck on more than one occasion, and the other men laughed as I scrambled away. He dragged me to the fights every week. He was drunk and loud, singing the common songs and calling out the names of the bears to the darkened houses along the way. Sackerson, the blind, eyes put out with a searing brand; Whiting and Stone, the twins; and behemoth, Harry Hunks, a god in fur.

The bears were chained outside the city in a gray piece of fallow known as the Gardens. Vendors in makeshift tents sold everything from salted meat to ancient sex magazines. Girls from long ago posed in those pages, chins jutting, hands on hips, skin faded to a viral green. Sometimes I pretended the girls could see us, just as we could see them, and I wondered what they must make of such foul and shambling wrecks.

My father often made me ride his shoulders on our passage through the city. One day I fell because he lurched so madly. I cut my cheek on a sharp rock. He dragged me all the way to the Gardens like that. I stood on our usual bench, blood trickling down my face. A woman said: "Don't let Sackerson smell you, boy. He'll pull his chain right out of the ground." She handed me a dirty pink handkerchief stitched with roses. I pressed it to my wound.

That was the day I met Hounds, the Bear Master's son. I'd seen him before, of course. Everyone who went to the Gardens had. He was usually too busy emptying barrels and carrying heavy pieces of cage to bother with talking to anyone, especially someone like me—the half-grown son of a Munsen Man. Women were never shy about sliding their hands over Hounds' shoulders as he passed through the crowd. And though he didn't seem to mind the attention, the most they ever got in return was a smile. Men admired Hounds too and were quick to make a drunken joke, which Hounds only sometimes rewarded with a chuckle. His face was plain and square. His body was big as a man's. Pierced through Hounds' left eyebrow was a piece of metal shaped like a tiny barbed hook.

Hounds stopped on his way through the crowd when he saw me holding the woman's flowered handkerchief to my face. "Fancy," he said.

I pulled the handkerchief away so as not to look like such a fool.

"Better put it back," Hounds said. "You might bleed to death."

I didn't know how to respond.

"You come here to watch this sick show?" Hounds asked.

"My dad," I said without considering how childish I sounded, "he makes me."

"Yeah," Hounds said. "My dad makes me too, I guess."

Then Hounds' father was calling him.

Hounds took his leave with barely a nod.

2.

When we got home, my older sister, June, told my father he was reckless for dragging me through the city with a cut on my face. She was tall and sickly, with stringy hair and bluish-white skin. "And what's this filthy thing?" she said, pointing at the pink handkerchief.

Father didn't listen to June. He never did. Instead, he went out to comb the yard for artifacts. When June and I were alone in the kitchen, I said, "I spoke to someone today."

June's frown looked like Mother's. "Who, Freddy?" she asked.

"The Bear Master's son," I said, "called Hounds."

"That's not a name."

I shrugged. "It's what he calls himself. He's handsome, June."

"Handsome how?"

"Big, with a good face. You should meet him," I said. "I could take you to the Gardens."

June turned her back on me and started cutting a colorless pile of vegetables for dinner. "Don't let Mayor Munsen find out you have thoughts like that."

"Shut up," I said. "You think too much about the stupid mayor."

June looked hurt. And I was sorry for that.

"He might be the one who saves us," June said. "He might be the only one who can."

3.

That evening after dinner, June and I played a game. She covered my eyes with her cool, damp hands and asked me to remember what was in the room. "Black stove," I said. "Coal bucket. Wooden table. Chairs. Painting of a man with a donkey."

"Is that all?" she said.

"That's all."

"Did you see Mother standing there?"

"Of course not, June."

"Then you aren't looking hard enough, Freddy."

That's how she acted too. Like we weren't all alone in the house. Like Mother was still alive.

"How much of Mother do you remember?" June asked.

"Nothing," I said. "Just her face."

That was a lie told for June's benefit. My sister was strong, yet there were times she needed my protection. What I actually remembered was the way Mother died. As June told it, Mother had expired from a disease. And I suppose it might have looked like that to someone who found her lying on the floor. But I saw what *actually* happened. I couldn't have been older than four or five. Mother fell to the floor, long dress tangled about her legs, hands kneading her gut like she was in pain. June was at the market. Father was at work. Mother called out the names of objects, most of which I didn't recognize: electric razor, tissue paper, light bulb, filing cabinet. Mother had a habit of making these sorts of lists. Mainly she taught her lists to June, telling her that as long as we remembered the names of objects we'd never be entirely lost. Neither June nor I fully understood what she meant by *lost*.

Mother wound her fingers through the bars of my crib and pulled herself up to look at me. "Keyboard," she whispered, "lava lamp, tennis shoe, my little boy." She put her hand on my leg, squeezing too tightly. Then she started to cough, hard enough to shake the crib. That's when the walls and floor began to darken. Like Mother was somehow dislodging shadows from her lungs.

I remember thinking we weren't alone anymore once she started coughing. There were people in the walls and in the floor. Over the years, I've considered that these people might have been an invention of a mind too young to cope with a mother's dying. Like how others believe they've seen angels after a public burning. But I don't think I made them up. There *were* bodies there in the half-light, figures without features, figures in strange clothing, leaning in to get a better look at Mother's death. One of them even seemed to show concern, coming close to the bed where I lay. And though I couldn't see a face, I knew it was a woman from her shape. The shadow-woman cared about me. She seemed frightened for me. Then Mother was dead, her nose pressed flat against the floor like a nail not yet driven. The figures were gone too. And I was left alone.

4.

As I said before, Father was a Munsen Man, named after our new mayor who'd run on a ticket of reform. Munsen wore fine dark suits and used what he called "classic rhetorical hand gestures" to emphasize his words. He said soon the city gates would all be open once again, and he held a fist above his palm to make it seem true. The fallows, he said, would be cleansed— hands clasped gently in front of his chest. Every house

would have electricity—palms open. Even the fallows
would have electricity—palms still open. There would
be no lack of food—hands prone, folded. The sick would
be healed—fingers splayed, held high. And we would
all learn the truth of our existence—a closed fist of re-
assurance. "Our dreadful night is nearly done, my fel-
lows," Munsen intoned with his fingers lightly steepled.
Everyone cheered for him in the same way they'd once
cheered for a hanging.

Father traveled the city in an orange horse cart,
trying to clean the uncleanable for Mayor Munsen. He
often found treasures like his "maniacal" pencil (a yellow
tube that sprouted lead when you pushed on its eraser).
Father brought his treasures home, hiding them in the
house or even going as far as burying them in the yard.
June retrieved the objects after Father had fallen asleep
and tried to teach me lessons. We sat at the kitchen
table, the surface of which was warped. It looked like
water's waves. She'd put her cool fingers over mine and
say, "Freddy, this is important. Mother taught me, and
she would have wanted you to know too. We have to
remember the names because they keep us tethered
to what's real. That's what she told me. Father thinks
these things are magic. That's why he's lost. This is just
a thimble, used for protection during sewing. And this
one is called a paper's clip, used for binding surplus.
And this one," June held up a flat chunk of plastic with
numbered buttons on its surface, "was once a piece of a
*telio*phone for talking, using networks of the air."

I turned the fragment of the teliophone over and
looked at it. Then I put the thimble on top of it like a small
hat. "Why don't we use these things anymore, June?"

June paused. "I don't know if we ever used them,"

she said. "Maybe they leaked in from somewhere else."
She looked downtrodden. "I should have asked Mother."
I wanted to touch her hand, but I knew I shouldn't.
She didn't like to be touched. June had a fear of disease.
She turned her face from mine. She closed her eyes.
"I'm sorry," she said. "I was older. I should have known."

5.

Hounds and I met again at a water barrel near the
salted meat tent. Father had dragged me to the Gardens
more often than usual that week. Hounds drank from
a rusty ladle, then offered water to me. And though it
smelled of iron, I drank heartily, if only to linger there.
Hounds said, "We both got shit for fathers, Freddy. Ev-
erybody's got shit for fathers, but you and I got the worst
of the shit, you know that?"

"I know," I said.

"You're a good listener," Hounds said. "Most people
who got shit for fathers are good listeners. You know
that too?"

I nodded.

Because there was no work for him, Hounds and I
left the Gardens that day and lay in an open field to the
west. We were far enough away from the bears that the
cheering crowd sounded like wind. My father was drunk.
I knew he wouldn't miss me. On the horizon stood four
buildings, colored the same dirty white as the sky. Their
windows were shattered and looked like toothy mouths.
On the one closest to me, I could read a name stamped
out in large blue letters: *Sanaco 1*—a word that meant
nothing, though it must have meant a great deal once
to have been written so large. The other buildings, I assumed, were connected to the first, making them Sanaco

2, 3, and 4. These buildings were not part of the city. They were in the fallows, the spoiled land that Mayor Munsen promised to cleanse and reclaim. Hounds said his father told him the buildings had once been offices where people did business. I told him about thimbles and papers clips and teliophones of the air. He said all those things had probably been used in the offices once. When I asked him how he knew, he said, "I went over there to explore awhile back. I was sick of my dad's shit and wanted to get away."

"What did you see, Hounds?" I said, propping myself up on my elbow to look into his black eyes. I watched the muted afternoon light glint off the metal hook pierced through his eyebrow.

"Everything," he said. "Piles and piles of fucking everything."

"Artifacts?"

"Unnamed stuff," he said.

"I bet my ma could have named those things," I said. "She knew all the old names."

Hounds considered this, and I hoped he might ask about my mother. The idea of telling him the story of the people who'd come from the walls and floor when she died excited me. I wanted him to know my secrets. But in the end, he didn't ask.

"You want to go to Sanaco, Hounds?" I said. "Maybe look around together? I can tell you if I recognize anything."

He shook his head. "Not the kind of place I'd go twice, Freddy. There was something wrong in there."

"Wrong how?"

"The air inside was all dark, even though the sun came in through the broken windows. It was like the night had swelled up behind the day, you know what I mean? Like when you can see sickness under somebody's skin. I kept feeling like I was going to fall down a hole, but there *weren't* any holes. I had to steady myself, hold onto the wall—only the wall felt soft, like melted cheese. Like my hand might push right through it."

"Was anybody in there?" I said.

He didn't answer for a long time, then said, "I think maybe there was. But it wasn't the kind of somebody that you or I could talk to."

6.

Mostly, Hounds didn't want to talk about Sanaco. He wanted to talk about fathers. He said that bearbaiting, his own father's profession, was the sort of fucked-up thing that only human beings could invent. "When this place belongs to me," Hounds said, "and it's all *gonna* belong to me one day, I'll turn it into a fucking parkland, someplace with paths where people can walk around decent-like and think, without all this shitting noise. In the middle of it all, maybe I'll dig a big lake and put up a goddamned statue and write all the bears' names on its chest: Sackerson, Whiting, and Stone, and fucking Harry Hunks. I'll even write the names of the bears that died if I can remember. There used to be one called Tangle Root, you know—got her guts gnawed out by a dog. We didn't even know she was pregnant till she was killed. And I won't say that nobody was blind nor twins nor god of the stupid bears."

"How'd the bears get those names anyway?" I asked.

"My old man found them in some book," he said. "A fucked-up book of theatricals."

I didn't know what a theatrical was. Hounds told me

it was a sort of thing where people pretended they had lives that made sense. They acted out characters who moved along the line of a story. He said people didn't put on theatricals anymore because no one believed that life *had* a proper story. "They'd rather see a bear bite a fucking dog in the ass," he scoffed. "And that's not a plot. That's no fucking plot at all, Freddy."

7.

Bearbaiting worked like this—a bear was chained to a stake in the middle of the gravel circle, then two dogs were set loose upon it. Only two at first, to make the fight fair. The bear tried to stand. It swung and roared at the dogs whose jaws dripped foam as they bit the bear and dodged the massive paws until everyone on the raised benches around the arena had nearly fallen down from cheering. Once in a while, a third dog was released if the bear seemed to be too much in control. By the end of a fight, both bear and dogs alike were wet with blood. Fur stood in matted spikes. Blood ran from mouths and noses. The bears made such impotent and furious sounds that I had to cover my ears. And the dogs sounded even worse. I never knew a dog could scream until I went to the Gardens.

Hounds told me a secret as we lay on our backs in the fallows one day, ringed by the pale offices of Sanaco. I was rambling about some rumors I'd heard about Mayor Munsen. People loved to gossip about him, especially at the Gardens. They said he hadn't been born in the city at all—that he really didn't even know that much about our city. He came from a place where classic hand gestures weren't uncommon and everyone wore suits like he wore, blue suits with necker-ties. Some people even said that Mayor Munsen wasn't *supposed* to be in our city. His coming was against the rules. Though when asked what rules they were speaking of, they said they didn't know. Hounds seemed distant as I spoke. He stared off into the trees around Sanaco. And just when I started talking about going against the rules, he broke in with a secret. "I'm gonna let 'em all go," he said.

"Let what go?" I said.

"The bears," he replied, "all the bears."

I propped myself up, looking into his face. The bluish sun glinted off the hook in his eyebrow. "Your dad would kill you, Hounds."

"The old man won't have a chance."

The breeze seemed colder then. I felt suddenly exposed there in the grass. The fallows were a dangerous place. There were people who sometimes hunted there with crossbows or came to do other things not legal within the walls of the city. Normally, I felt protected when I was with Hounds, but at that moment I understood he was not there to protect me. He was there to consider his plans.

"You're going to let the bears run off at night?" I asked.

"No," he said, "during one of the fights. I already figured out a way to fix the collar, the rest will just be a matter of opening cages."

I looked down the length of him, my gaze settling on the scuffed wooden heels of his boots. He often used his boot heels to hammer cage stakes into the ground.

"The bears will hurt people," I said.

"Don't all these people deserve to be hurt, Freddy? Haven't the bears been hurt so much that we can't even look at them anymore?"

I pictured the crowd at the Gardens—all those mismatched, tired faces, the jumble of salvaged clothes. I pictured them running from Sackerson, from Harry Hunks and the twins. "Your dad will just get more bears," I said.

"He can't," Hounds said. "The man who got these for us died. There's no one else who even knows where there are wild bears anymore. Hopefully, they'll kill my old man first, anyway."

"You mean that, Hounds?"

He acted like he didn't hear. "I don't want you to get hurt though," he said. "I'll signal to you somehow, let you know to get away. I'll touch this—" Hounds put his finger on the hook above his eyebrow. "You can take your father with you if you want."

Hounds' revelation made me strangely bold. Maybe it was because death hung in the air around us. Maybe it was because I was so scared. In my mind, the crowd was already being torn apart, and I reached out and put my hand on Hounds' smooth forearm, something I'd never dared before. His skin was warm. I could feel his blood beating beneath.

"Don't do this," I said.

Hounds turned slowly to look at me, and then carefully, delicately almost, he pulled his arm away.

"Sorry," I said. "Sorry, Hounds. I was just feeling—"

Hounds stood and dusted his jeans, an action which seemed to take forever. "You just surprised me is all, Fred," he said finally. "People touch me. They always do, and I never know why. I just thought you were different is all."

8.

Maybe June's change of heart about going to the Gardens came from the fact that Mayor Munsen announced his intention to tour the fallows as part of his promised Investigations and Reforms program. June approved of the mayor greatly. She kept a drawing of him in her bedroom. Or maybe the change came merely from a new artifact Father had found: a transparent rubber breathing mask with two silver filters meant to siphon air.

A cold fear spiked my gut as I watched June descend the stairs on the day of the fights. Her long white dress brushed the toes of her walking boots. And the rubber breathing mask glittered like a jewel over her mouth and nose.

"June—what are you doing?" I said.

She smiled at me through the clear rubber mask. "You always wanted me to get out of the house, Freddy."

"Something's going to happen, June, sometime soon," I said, thinking of Hounds' plan. "And I don't want—"

At that point, my father came in, loud in his work boots. He stared at June, pointing his maniacal pencil at her like a scepter. "You're wearing my property, girl," he said.

She smiled at him. I'd never seen June smile so much. "That's right, Daddy. And if you shut up about it, I'll sing your stupid bear songs with you on the way to the show. How about that?"

The three of us became an odd procession, passing under Ethelsgate, singing together about Sackerson the blind and Harry Hunks the marauding god while my father made triangles in the air with his pencil, as if directing a marching band.

9.

The Gardens was packed that day. I only got glimpses of Mayor Munsen in his dark suit and necker-tie, gray hair rippling back from his brow in an elegant display. He made his famous gestures as he passed through the crowds, speaking to what he called his "citizens." Even in that drunken turmoil, Munsen held sway, believing so firmly in order that everyone around him momentarily believed in it too. A fight broke out between two filth-covered men, and Munsen simply walked over to them, put his hands on their shoulders, and asked them to be brothers, which, amazingly, caused them to stop.

June nearly swooned at this. "The mayor's going to surprise us," she said. "He'll show us how to change. Maybe even today."

"I don't think the mayor understands anything about change," I said darkly, scanning the crowd for Hounds.

The bear scheduled to compete that day was Harry Hunks, which made sense. Only the biggest and the best for Mayor Munsen. God of the people should meet god of the bears. When the Bear Master's men led Harry forth, my flesh turned cold. One of his paws was the size of my head, and one of his black eyes was the size of my open mouth. A cloud of flies traveled with him, and he swung his big head from left to right, trying to knock the buzzing creatures away. The men held him in pole-harnesses while Hounds worked to fasten the collar at its maximum extension around the bear's thick neck. When Hounds was done, he turned and seemed to see me in the crowd. My father and I always sat in the same spot, low and to the left, for better view of the ring. Blood sometimes fell on us like rain. Hounds did not nod or gesture. He only stared, perhaps remembering how I'd touched him in the fallows. The hook above his eye glittered. And I was seized by fear.

"Is that the one you like?" June asked, the sound of her voice muffled by the rubber breathing mask. "He *is* attractive, Freddy."

This was the day. Of course, it was. Munsen was here. The crowd was larger. This was the best day to let them go.

"June," I yelled above the cheers, grabbing her hand, "We have to go."

June craned her neck, searching for Munsen, stopping only long enough to say, "Don't be stupid. I haven't had my chance to talk to the mayor yet. I want to wait until after he sees the fight."

"There isn't going to be a fight," I yelled, pulling at her.

I looked back toward Hounds. He was gone. And something had spooked the Bear Master's men.

A woman holding a jaundiced baby started to scream. I turned to see blind Sackerson rise from the crowd, nostrils flaring, jaws agape. His eyes were nothing but two hairy slits in his skull. Sackerson stood on two legs and roared, and at first people seemed unable to comprehend what was happening. This was Sackerson, after all. Sacred Son. They'd watched him week after week from afar, and yet now he stood among them, close enough to smell his barn rot and see the shining insects in his hair.

"Fucking shit," my father yelled, standing from the bench and dropping the maniacal pencil.

Sackerson reached forward with one big paw, taking a chunk out of the screaming woman's face. The bloody hole seemed a second mouth, also screaming. Amazingly she held onto the baby, crushing it to her chest as she backed away. I finally managed to pull June out of her seat. Her body had gone stiff. "Freddy," she said, "what—"

"Don't talk," I yelled. "No time."

And then we both saw Munsen himself, pushed by the swell of the crowd into the arena where Stone, newly escaped from his own cage, towered. The bear swayed and Munsen swayed. Munsen's mouth hung open in surprise. Then in a single smooth motion, Stone took Munsen's lower jaw off his face, and the mayor was suddenly a fountain of his own blood. His orating hands hung limp at his sides. His fine necker-tie became a sluiceway. He remained, silently staring at us all for a moment, and then a sound rose from the exposed hole of his throat, louder than all the other screams in the crowd put together. The sound increased to a near-inhuman volume. It was such a frightening noise. Even Stone was momentarily stunned. Munsen's body had become a siren, transmitting a final message. *He wasn't from the city. He didn't belong in the city. How had the city done this to him?* And then Stone was on the mayor, tearing.

"Run," I yelled to June before I saw the crowd had already swept her away. I panicked, fighting bodies to look for her. And finally I saw. June had been pushed from the arena and was running across the fallows toward the four white office buildings that stood in a half-circle, faster than I'd ever seen her run, white dress raised above her knees, hair snapping against the wind. She was closely pursued by the vast form of Hairy Hunks, god of the bears. His oceans of flesh rose and fell as he bounded, front legs leaving the ground, then back legs, roaring at June in excitement. Half the metal collar still hung from his neck.

Without pause, I scooped up Father's maniacal pencil because it was the only thing within reach that might be useful as a weapon, and as the crowd fell away, I raced after her. June slammed through the glass bank of doors on Sanaco 1 at the far end of the fallows. Harry Hunks shattered the glass as he shoved his body through the entrance. A lifetime seemed to pass as I ran, moving across the fallows, breath scorching my chest. Screams rose from the Gardens behind me, but Sanaco 1 was silent, all cracked walls and broken windows, blue letters hanging from the side. I hoped this place was not June's tomb. I had time to wonder about my father. Had he been killed? And Hounds—where had he gone after he'd set loose the bears? Then I was at the broken door, refusing to slow as I crossed the threshold.

10.

It's hard to find the language to explain what I found in the lobby of Sanaco 1. Spaces in the city were built on a human scale and were meant to house humble acts of living. The largest room I'd ever been in was the dining hall at a local eating house called the Golden Stag, but that was dwarfed by Sanaco's lobby. At first, the space struck me as not a room at all, but a new kind of outdoors. There was no end—just a cold sprawl of white and gray tile, buckled in places from what looked like old flood damage. Plants had broken through the floor, long weedy growths that had turned white from lack of sun. Water stains ran down the walls, and great banks of lights had fallen from the ceiling, shattering to pieces among the plants. A mechanical staircase rose from the center of the lobby, leading up to what appeared to be a second level with a floor of glass. And when I looked at the staircase, I thought *escalator*, though I'd certainly never heard that word before. At a different moment, this kind of word salvage would have driven me mad. How did I know the names of objects that I had no reference for? Had Mother filled my head with names before I could even speak, and now they bubbled up from the cracks?

"Escalator!" I yelled at the metal staircase, though I'd intended to call my sister's name. Neither June nor Harry Hunks was in the lobby. All remained silent. And then from down a long, broken hall behind the escalator came the echo of sharp footfalls. A woman appeared in the distance, and I nearly forgot why I was in Sanaco 1, despite the desperate situation June was in. The woman's black hair was folded into a careful bun, and she wore a pair of clear plastic eyeglasses that reminded me of June's breathing mask. Her suit was of the same quality as Munsen's, undamaged and whole. And instead of looking at me, she read through a thick sheaf of papers as she walked, as though she weren't afraid of tripping over the debris or plant life in the lobby. As though those things weren't even there.

"Mamma," I said, because that's who it was. It was Mother walking toward me. Yet somehow death had changed her, washed her clean. "Where's June?" I yelled, feeling an emotion almost like joy.

Mother looked up sharply, surprised by my voice, and though she was still some distance away, she said, "How did you get in here?"

She didn't recognize me. That much was clear.

She had no idea who she was talking to. I was just

a meaningless filth-covered boy standing in the ruined lobby.

"What happened?" I said, running toward her, and when I got close enough, when she saw my face, a wave of what looked like nausea passed over her.

"How?" she said again.

"I'm looking for June," I said. "June came here."

The name of her daughter seemed to register, though not in the way it should have. It was more like she'd heard the name long ago. The name was a piece of flickering memory. She sifted through her papers, reading until she found the proper one. Mother read it twice, lips moving, before saying, "June was killed by a bear."

My throat tightened. "Where?" I said, looking again at the emptiness of the lobby.

She read further. "The Gardens," she said, "near where she was seated with her father and her brother. Her brother held her head while she died—" Mother looked up slowly. "Freddy?"

"Of course I'm *Freddy*! Don't you remember? What happened to you, Mamma?"

Her hand went to her face, exploring the ridge of her eyebrow, the edge of her mouth. "They used my image," she said, more to herself than to me, "my face. They thought it would be—funny, I suppose."

"What does that mean? Funny how?" I said, growing angrier now, thinking of June alone somewhere in the awful white monster of a building—alone and afraid, pursued by Harry Hunks.

Mother—except she wasn't Mother—"the woman" put her papers on the floor and got to her knee in front of me. "My name is Rebecca Stroughton," she said. "What was your mother's name?"

"Her name was Mother," I said, feeling sick with confusion. "Your name is Mother. Mamma."

She closed her eyes. "And what is your surname, Freddy? What name do we share?"

I didn't know what a surname was, so I didn't answer. Instead, I scanned the room again, wondering if June had somehow made it up the silver escalator. "I was at the Gardens," I said, careful with my words, wanting this woman to understand. "Hounds set loose the bears, and one of them killed Munsen while one of them went after June—"

The mayor's name appeared to register. "*Munsen* caused this?" she said.

"The mayor."

"He isn't a mayor. He's just a man who never wanted to play properly."

"Play what?"

Rebecca Stroughton took a breath. "I sat with you when she died—the woman who looked like me. I sat with you, and I even cried for you. Everyone thought it was ridiculous that I should cry over something like that. But you were so tiny there in your crib—so real.

"Real?" I said.

"You had to see her die. So you would form a certain bond with your sister. That was their reasoning, as much as there's a proper reason for anything. Someone thought it was a good idea. 'Let's see how he grows up if he watches his mother die.' That was how someone decided to play."

"Stop saying 'play!'" I yelled, backing away from her. "What does *play* mean? What does 'real' mean?"

Rebecca Stroughton reached out. I didn't want to be touched by her. And then, from some distant corner of Sanaco 1, I heard June. She screamed. Then came a roar from Harry Hunks. The world, which had been sinking quickly into shadow, slammed suddenly back into focus.

"Freddy, don't!" the woman with the Mother face yelled. "There's no one up there." But I ran from her, up the escalator, taking two metal stairs at a time, following the sound of June's voice.

11.

I'm not sure when I gave up searching. It's strange to think that a place could be as big as Sanaco 1. So many empty rooms. No artifacts. Nothing to name. It was big enough to lose a sister. Even big enough to lose the god of the bears. I've tried telling myself that June's screams, the ones I heard so clearly when I stood in the lobby with Rebecca Stroughton, might have been old echoes, ghosts of sound. But even ghosts are too much to ask for in a place like this. The walls aren't even soft like Hounds said. No, the walls *flicker*. And the worst part, the very worst part—there's nothing behind those walls, not even darkness.

I stopped looking for June. I clicked the pink eraser of my father's maniacal pencil, releasing lead from the tip. I found a good long space of wall—one that wasn't flickering (at least not yet)—and I began to write, hoping that one day someone from the city would find my writing. Maybe even Hounds would find it, if he ever realized what he did was wrong.

Maybe Hounds will read this and know something of what happened. How June got lost. How I got lost. How the walls started to flicker and fade. And I couldn't find my way back downstairs again.

I think the lead is running out now.

I've clicked the eraser too many times.

I should stop writing, but I'm afraid because I'm almost certain that when I stop, Rebecca Stroughton will be proven right. That's why her mother-face looked so sad. She knew. It was clear to her. There isn't anyone up here. Not even me.

The Re'em

Upon the death of German monk Ulrich Gottard (drowned in the pale and churning waters of the River Lech), a manuscript is delivered to the Roman Curia for consideration by the Holy See. Lord Protector of Cromberg Cloister, Father Benedict, writes in his letter of submittal that he deems the document a distressing epistle due, in part, to its bizarre and heretical nature. "It is most certainly a *renunciation*," Benedict writes, "however unusual, however obscure." What is perhaps most troubling to the Lord Protector though is the reaction the manuscript incites among the younger initiates of his German cloister. Like the drowned monk himself, these youths are said to be delicate and romantic. "Troublesome searchers," Benedict calls them, "the sort that might wipe tears from their eyes at Matins." He notes that these "followers" of Gottard began to meet secretly in a dimly lit chamber beneath the cloister's chapter hall. It was there they attempted an interpretation of the manuscript, treating its passages as if they were some holy writ. The group began referring to itself as the "Re'em." "These boys cling to one another," Father Benedict writes. "They hold each other in such dreadful high esteem. And together, they find meaning where meaning is not."

The narrative set forth in Ulrich Gottard's manuscript—now well known in higher echelons of the Roman Church—unfolds over a series of days during a visit to the Holy Land soon after his taking of First Orders. An amateur geologist as well as a man of God, Gottard begins his writings with a description of certain curious formations of volcanic alkaline rock in the arid landscape surrounding Mount Sinai in Egypt. Gottard notes that the rocks had, in places, fused together and formed what looked like the arches of a "black and imposing architecture, crumbling on the stony hillside—as if left there by some ancient and unknown race."

It was in one such glittering vault of blackish stone Gottard encountered the creature that would soon overwhelm his thoughts, as well as the thoughts of his future acolytes. "The animal stood upon its four legs," Gottard writes, "and was the size and approximate shape of a Calabrese stallion. Its coat was pale in color. The hair of its pelt was longish, matted. This was not a domesticated beast, and yet its state did not bespeak brutishness either."

Other attributes of the animal's appearance were entirely unique. For unlike a horse, the creature was possessed of a cloven hoof and a short leathery tail. It watched the monk's approach with a serene and thoughtful gaze, "as a sovereign might regard his subject." The creature's most striking feature was the single braided horn that protruded from the center of its head. "The horn," Gottard writes, "in certain light, appeared semitranslucent and at other times, looked as though it was made of stone. There were even moments it gleamed, as if forged of silver." The monk soon begins referring to the creature as a "re'em"—an animal mentioned in the Vulgate of St. Jerome (*Canst thou bind the horned re'em with his band in the furrow? Or will he harrow the valley after thee?*)

Upon returning to the village near the mountain, Gottard ascertained that such creatures, though uncommon, were at times sighted in the area. Their home—a valley some distance west of Mount Sinai—was accessible if accompanied by a suitable guide. Gottard, unable to banish the strange encounter from his thoughts, produced coins from his purse, and a guide was brought forth: a tall young man, dressed in white linen, introduced only as Chaths.

Gottard writes that, upon seeing the young man for the first time, he felt what might well be called an uncanny sense of recognition. It was not that Gottard had met the guide before, but in Chaths he saw something of himself. "He did not resemble me in appearance. His eyes were dark. His brow, delicate and smooth. Yet all the while, I felt as though the villagers had produced, not a guide for me but a mirror. There was some evident tether stretched between the two of us. It bound us, as a man's reflection is fastened to him but is never precisely the same as him."

Early the following morning, Gottard and Chaths set out to locate the valley of the re'em. They made their way through the rocky landscape, with Gottard stealing sidelong glances at this curious "mirror." The guide remained a silent presence. Any given query from Gottard produced, at most, a few mumbled phrases in Chath's own language. The journey lasted longer than the monk expected, and soon the guide indicated they should make camp for the night. This would allow them to arrive at the valley by morning light. "It would be unwise to approach after nightfall," Chaths said in words finally plain enough for Gottard to comprehend.

"Are there dangers?" Gottard asked.

"We are in the desert," Chaths replied. "There are always dangers."

Despite a long day of travel, the monk found he could not sleep. A wind called from the distant hills. Small animals scuttled in the shadows just beyond the reach of the firelight. Gottard spent much of the night considering patterns in the flames. He imagined he saw within them the re'em, walking in circles. Wherever the re'em trod, black formations of stone appeared to rise—elegant horns that pierced the earth. The creature shifted and turned in the light. It drew nearer, then moved farther away. The re'em no longer looked like a sovereign. Instead, it seemed to Gottard that he watched the dance of some ancient god.

After hours of this, the monk finally forced himself to turn from these visions. He regarded his sleeping guide and was surprised to find that the so-called mirror of the other man's face had changed during the night. There was now something in Chaths' features that reminded Gottard—not only of himself—but also of a boy called Aenor he'd known during his schooldays. Aenor had been a quiet sort, tall and thin, prone to exhaustion. He and Gottard often walked together along the stony banks of the River Lech. The boys skipped stones across the river's silt-white waters. They talked of the life of the soul. They would sometimes sit together beneath a crooked tree. Aenor would put his head on Gottard's shoulder, claiming he needed rest. Once, Aenor had taken Gottard's hand and said, "My mother says I am handsome. Do you think I am handsome as well, Ulrich?" Gottard did not know how to respond to such a question. He merely waited in silence, gazing out at the white River Lech. Finally, the silence itself became an answer.

⊠

The sun rose like a bronze seal above the desert. To Gottard, the white sky looked like the closed door of Heaven. The monk went to kneel at the edge of the firelight. He wanted to pray in order to soothe himself. His memories of Aenor troubled him. The boy had been gentle and so kind. Gottard told Aenor that he could not love him. He loved only God.

"I bowed my head," he writes. "As I began my prayers, I felt a terrible sensation. It was as if an invisible hand had pressed itself against the very surface of my soul. For the first time, my prayers felt as though they would not rise. They would not ascend the heavenly ladder. Instead, they remained trapped inside my own flesh. Confined in that prison."

This disturbance caused Gottard to call out, waking Chaths. The guide blinked at him in the morning light.

"Can you hear my voice, brother?" Gottard asked the guide. His voice was pleading.

"I hear you plainly," Chaths replied.

Gottard crossed himself. "And when I make the cross, can you see it?"

"I can see your gesture," Chaths said. He stood and brought water in a wooden cup. "You must drink."

Gottard did drink. He found he wanted to take Chaths' hand. He wanted to feel the warmth of the guide, the life of him. "I recognize something in you," he said.

"You should drink more water," Chaths replied.

"Please," the monk said. "You hold some secret."

Chaths knelt beside Gottard at the edge of the camp.

It was as if he too intended to pray. But instead, he only gazed out over the landscape that was covered in bluish rock. Finally, he said, "It's not an animal you seek, Brother Gottard. Not as you believe."

"What then?" Gottard asked.

The guide lowered his head.

"What else could it be?" Gottard asked again.

"The animal does not exist as other things do," the guide responded. "Sight of it is thought to be caused by a fissure that develops in the brain. A fever—"

Gottard remembered feeling ill a few nights before he encountered the re'em. He'd attributed the sickness merely to the sort of malaise that often came on during travel. "You're saying the creature is some kind of dream?" Gottard asked.

Chaths shook his head. "The fissure—it allows a man to see crossways. The animal walks there in that light."

"I don't understand. Crossways in the light?"

Chaths offered more water to the monk. "This will help. The water soothed me as well."

"You've been afflicted by the fever too?" Gottard asked.

Chaths nodded. "That is why I am to be your guide."

The idea that sickness had caused him to see the re'em troubled Gottard. Was it possible he chased some mirage? Was all of this a fool's errand? "If I am sick," he asked, "will I be cured?

Chaths looked at the monk solemnly. "There is no cure, Brother Gottard," he said. "There is only the valley."

Chaths indicated they should begin their journey before the sun rose too high above the mountains. Gottard did his best not to stumble upon the rocks as they walked. He felt ill from his sleeplessness. Perhaps, he thought, the fever might return. Soon, the two men came upon, not a valley, but a kind of tunnel in the low wall of a rocky outcropping. The same black volcanic stones that Gottard had seen upon his original encounter with the re'em surrounded the entrance to the tunnel. For a moment, the passage appeared to waver, fluctuating in shape and size. Gottard wondered if this anomaly was yet another symptom of the supposed fissure in the brain.

Chaths indicated that Gottard must be silent once they were inside the tunnel. The horned creatures were not easily disturbed, he said. But there were other things that lived in the valley beyond the tunnel. Things that did not appreciate the presence of men. The young guide seemed troubled as he spoke, as if he could perceive some future the monk could not. Gottard wanted to provide comfort to Chaths. He reached toward the guide. But the guide pulled away, indicating that Gottard was not to touch him once they were in the valley.

It is in Gottard's description of the valley that the sense of his manuscript begins to falter. For what he saw after emerging from the other side of the tunnel does not correlate to any known topography in the vicinity of Mount Sinai. "It was a landscape, verdant and lush," he writes. "Like a garden allowed to run wild. There were large bright flowers, maddening things with fleshlike petals as big as a man's hand, and springs that spilled forth miraculously from stone." Further along, the landscape began to change and the earth became covered with what Gottard describes as a new variety of rock. The monk posits that the pressure of ancient volcanic activity had caused crystals to form. The large crystals protruded from the earth and were of varying colors: deep vermilion, saffron, and azure. Sunlight streamed into the valley at an odd angle (crosswise, thought Gottard) striking the crystals and causing a prismatic effect.

The deeper Gottard and Chaths moved into the garden, the more it seemed as though they were walking on the floor of a strange inland sea. The waters of the sea were composed of wildly contrasting colors, so utterly immersive that Gottard soon began to feel as though he was drowning. He fell to his knees finally, and Chaths came to support him. Gathered in the guide's arms, Gottard forgot he'd been warned not to touch Chaths in the valley, and he put his hand on the young man's face and then on his neck. Chaths was beautiful in that moment. "Not like a mirror," Gottard writes. "He was entirely himself."

It was then that Gottard heard the sound of hoof on stone, and he turned to look out into the valley. Standing between two of the great crystalline formations that rose from the earth was the horse with the single horn. And yet, this was no horse. Gottard was now certain of that. The re'em approached the two men, lowering its head. Colors that rose from the surrounding crystals appeared to intensify. They shifted to paint the body of the pale beast. Gottard, in his delirium, believed that the horn itself began to bleed. He realized the protrusion was made of neither crystal nor bone. It was some form of condensed light. It ran in streams down the creature's face, filling its black and thoughtful eyes with color.

Gottard reached out to touch the braided horn (for the re'em was now close enough for him to do just that). Yet before he could touch the horn, he sensed a second approach. Chaths had said the re'em were not alone in the valley, and Gottard realized with great and trembling fear that this was true. The monk writes: "The be-ing—for it was a sort of being that approached—proved too large to actually be perceived by my eye. It seemed instead that the atmosphere, the very air of the valley, grew dense. And it also seemed that the being sang in a voice that was too loud to be heard by my ear. Yet I could sense the sound of it, nonetheless."

"What advances?" Gottard asked.

"I am sorry, Brother Gottard," Chaths replied.

"What do you mean you are sorry?" the monk asked, turning to look at his guide. The young man was alive with bleeding color. Light swam across his body. He stood with his palm against the neck of the re'em.

"You are not permitted," Chaths said.

Gottard felt a horror at this. For he wanted to understand this place, to understand the re'em. And even more, to understand Chaths himself. "Who grants such permission?" Gottard asked.

Chaths did not respond.

"It was then," Gottard writes, "that the approaching form—the great intelligence—enclosed me. I felt as if I was drawn up into the palm of a vast hand—a hand too large for me to see. Chaths watched from his place in the garden, as did the re'em. I was lifted high enough I could perceive the entirety of the valley. All of it was alive with maddening color. I saw the lush and fleshlike flowers shining. I saw a whole heard of re'em running—making rivers in the shifting light. I was drawn higher still, until I felt that I was being pulled out into the heavenly spheres. I could hear the spheres singing; they joined their voices with the voice of the great being. And still, I was drawn upward, toward the cold Empyrean itself. When finally I awoke, I found myself on the hillside where I'd first encountered the beast. I lay beneath the crumbling black architecture there, already forgetting the colors I'd seen. Such was the dullness of our world. I called out for Chaths. My call went unanswered. The guide had remained in the valley. Likely he'd known all along he would stay. Perhaps that was the fate of all guides. And there beneath the black rock, I fell into a new delirium. I dreamed that I too would one day guide someone to the valley. And then I would finally be permitted.

Metempsychosis

Vienna, Austria 1902

A traveling museum moves down the dim thoroughfares of Salzburg and Innsbruck, Eisenstadt and Enns. Tents unfold from black carriages after sunset. Canvas glows with lamplight. A carnival barker leans against a tall podium, the front of which is painted with a single, staring eye. The barker doesn't speak. He looks as though he's half inside a dream. A phonograph in the museum's entryway emits a crackling voice. It's a doctor making notes on a patient with a mysterious disease: "The subject reports a belief that she is, in fact, a machine. Life for her is a function of someone else's devising. Speech is scripted. Action, no longer spontaneous. [The record skips.] Each day, the subject claims it is as though she's been asked to play out a scene. When I inquire *who* has asked her to do such a thing, she will not reply."

After purchasing a ticket from the dreaming barker, patrons are confronted with the museum's curious exhibition. In an antechamber, there are six faceless statues, diminutive men like brown homunculi. A placard explains the statues were retrieved from tombs in ancient Egypt. Pharaonic priests once used them during a ceremony called "the opening of the mouth." The ritual was thought to bring clay bodies to life, and the statues acted as guardians of the temple's treasure.

A young female patron with a gathering of edelweiss in her hair leans close to her husband's ear and asks if he thinks the statues might *still* be alive. Perhaps they guard the museum's corridors at night. The husband takes his wife's hand and smiles into his black mustache. "This isn't a house of horrors, Annalise. It is merely a showing of history. A remembrance. Come along now. I'll protect you."

Deeper still, patrons encounter the automatic chess player of Johann Maelzel that famously toured the Americas in the middle years of the previous century. The author E. A. Poe wrote of it. The automaton is said to have played astonishing games of chess, besting even the most skilled of competitors. It is broken now, a wreck of rust and peeling paint. One of the chess player's eyes has fallen from its head; the other is nothing more than a staring silver orb.

Arnaud Eisler, a baker's son from Vienna, wanders the makeshift halls of the traveling museum, peering carefully into its cluttered and dimly lit chambers. He is admittedly not interested in the curious displays—the robot made of wood and leather that once belonged to a king of the Zhou Dynasty, the *Book of Stones* written by a Muslim priest that details how to fashion live snakes and scorpions from wax, or even the mechanical angel built during the Late Middle Ages that is said to turn its face always toward the sun. These are dust-ridden relics from another age. And Arnaud has only recently arrived in the fullness of his youth. He's far more interested in his search for beauty. And it's just that search that brought him inside the museum tonight. For, not more than ten minutes ago, Arnaud saw the handsomest of boys—a docent, according to the badge he wore—lingering at the museum's tented entryway. The docent was possessed of such striking beauty: thick dark hair, firmly parted, and queer, inquisitive eyes. He was dressed in a well-fitted suit and leather jackboots. He looked nothing like the rough boys of Vienna. The moment Arnaud saw the docent, he desired him. He thought that if he could encounter this vision inside the museum, perhaps they might strike up some conversation. One thing would lead to another. And if the docent was so inclined, they might share a kiss, as Arnaud had so recently done with the son of a traveling merchant. That young man had tasted like stale cigarettes and liquor. This docent, however, would certainly taste far sweeter.

Yet now that Arnaud has purchased a ticket from the gaunt, silent barker behind the podium and made his way inside the tent, he finds the docent has disappeared into the shadows. Arnaud quickly begins to feel as though he's lost in a system of nested dreams. In one alcove, he sees what appears to be a mechanical black monk that rolls its white eyes and strikes its chest with a wooden cross at timed intervals. There too is a Roman suit of armor that's said to be a metal soldier called Talus alongside a self-reading book belonging to Count Artois of Burgundy. The book drones endlessly in Latin, using a high tinny voice. Finally, there's a mechanical bird with silver plumage and opal eyes displayed beneath a dome of glass. A placard explains that the Greek inventor Asclepius fashioned the bird. When wound, it is said to possess the ability to lead its owner to the very gates of Heaven.

Arnaud leans against the pedestal. "Damned fowl," he whispers. He should have gone to the tavern tonight or even to the stables where other young men are known to meet. He would have been guaranteed a kiss at least, even if it weren't from the one he so greatly desires. It's then that a voice behind him says, "Well now . . . what are your interests here?" Arnaud turns to see the dark-haired docent who's miraculously appeared from behind a black curtain. The boy is taller than Arnaud first believed. He has a faint yet pleasing accent. There's a distinct smell about him too, eucalyptus mixed with the tang of sweat. Arnaud's face feels hot. He's afraid he's blushing. But then again, the flickering lamplight in the chamber is so dim he doesn't think the boy will see.

"Interests?" Arnaud says.

The docent comes closer, wearing half a smirk. He adjusts the lapels of his own trim suit. "What have you come to see?"

Arnaud looks at the metal bird—the mechanical guide to Heaven. He thinks of all the exhibits he's encountered so far and finds he doesn't know how to respond. "Have you ever wound the bird?" he asks.

The docent shakes his head. "The key's lost. All the keys are lost. So say the proprietors."

"I didn't know the traveling museum was coming," Arnaud says. "There were no fliers in the square."

"No," the docent says. "I don't suppose there were."

Arnaud realizes he's already straining for a topic. Not a good sign. He came inside wanting to charm this boy, but now it's as if his thoughts labor under the weight of some spell. He's reminded of the heat in his own father's bakery, the way it can make him feel light-headed in the late afternoon. "What's the museum called then?" he asks finally.

"Doesn't have a name," the docent replies.

"Everything has a name," Arnaud says.

"It just a place where people come," the docent says, "for one reason or another. They find us."

"And who are these proprietors?" Arnaud asks. "Who do you work for?"

The docent's lips are thin and pale, yet somehow still seem exceedingly sensual. "Do you want to take a walk?" he asks. "I can show you some things if you like."

Arnaud nods. Of course he wants to take a walk. And he follows the docent down a dim hall, admiring the slope of the boy's shoulders and the narrowness of his waist. They soon pause to consider what appears to be a body beneath a sheet on a table. A placard nearby simply reads: "The Resurrection." The body begins to move haltingly and make a coughing noise as if trying to clear liquid from its throat. The docent pulls at Arnaud's sleeve. "Better not to look at this one for too long, I think."

The deeper the two boys move, the more Arnaud feels that he is missing some significant component of the traveling museum—a clue that would unlock the meaning of this place. He doesn't understand how the museum is organized, or even *if* it's organized. In one room, there's a porcelain doll that laughs, showing tiny pearllike teeth. In another, there's a shriveled brown hand that's said to come to life once every thousand years. There's a mirror that reflects a human shadow, yet no one is standing in front of it. Across the hall, there's a chamber that, through some trick of light, appears to contain an entire ocean.

"My name is Arnaud Eisler," Arnaud says as they walk. "Would you tell me your name?"

"I don't have one, I'm afraid," the docent says.

Now Arnaud feels as though he's being teased. Perhaps the docent can smell the bakery flour on Arnaud's clothing. Perhaps the docent thinks he is some country fool. "No name?" Arnaud says. "Just like the exhibition, eh?"

"Not exactly like that," the docent says. "I had a name once, I suppose. I just forgot it. Too much traveling, you see." He turns and winks at Arnaud.

There is very little conversation after that. They come to another phonograph like the one in the entryway. This one plays a recording of a man who's supposedly been dead for twelve days and has recently awakened. In a halting, weak voice that is oddly pitched, the man tells of the places he visited in death. "There was a garden," he says, "where souls changed form. Men became animals and animals, men. Some of the souls left the garden. They moved up like stars."

"Maybe we could go to a café," Arnaud offers. "Have a coffee? A glass of wine?"

"Difficult to get away," the docent says.

Arnaud clears his throat. He wants to ask questions: *Do you like to touch? Are you interested in boys?* Instead, he decides on a safer line. "So, where do you come from?" he asks. "Where did the exhibition begin?"

The docent looks distant, as if trying to recall. "There's just one more thing I think you should see," he says finally. "It's what most people come for, even though they don't always know it. Follow me."

Arnaud actually considers declining the offer. This whole experience has been so improbable. So unexpected. He realizes he isn't even likely to get that kiss. But then he looks at the docent again, appreciating the way the boy tilts his head as he waits in the doorway.

"Why not," Arnaud says. "Lead on."

As they walk, Arnaud sees indistinct bodies in the shadows up ahead that seem to swell and diminish. He wonders if these are other patrons or perhaps something else that wanders here in the museum. Arnaud realizes that he's a wandering shadow now too. He and the lovely docent. He thinks of his mother and father who are, at that moment, likely waiting for him in the warm rooms above the bakery. His father will be reading from the Bible. His mother will sit in a chair and peer out through the high window. Some part of him wishes he were there. He'd tell them the story of the museum, how strange it all was.

"Just down here," the docent says. And surprisingly, a staircase appears before them. *A staircase in a tent?* Arnaud thinks. *That isn't possible.* And yet they are descending.

"The proprietors are of the belief," the docent is saying, "that the whole cosmos is a clockwork. We are all pieces in its mechanism. They've invented a model of—well—you'll see."

At the bottom of the staircase, it's so dark that Arnaud can't see anything. He feels the docent's fingers brush his hand and draws back. The boy is cold, impossibly so.

"Maybe we shouldn't—" Arnaud says.

"What's wrong?" the docent asks.

"Nothing," Arnaud replies. "I only want a cigarette."

The boy is so close now that Arnaud thinks he should be able to feel his breath. Yet there's nothing. "It's just up ahead," the docent says. And before Arnaud can ask any more questions, they're moving once again. Down a twisting corridor that looks as though it's been hewn from the earth itself. *We're in a cave,* Arnaud thinks. But he knows that's ridiculous, of course. This isn't a cave. It's another part of the traveling museum, another illusion in this collection of illusions.

And then Arnaud sees it there in the half-light—what appears to be a full-sized clockwork man. The clockwork crawls in the dust of the cavern floor, making odd stiff movements with its hands, as if searching for something.

"Go ahead," the docent says. "Have a look."

As Arnaud approaches, he recognizes the figure's clothes: brown trousers and a loose cotton shirt, common clothes, dappled with flour. The android's hair is dun-colored. And the face—Arnaud has seen that wide, square face in his own shaving glass. For there, crawling in the dust of the cavern floor, is Arnaud himself. Only it's not him. This is some copy, some piece of metal brought to life.

"The proprietors," the docent says, "are building a cosmos within the cosmos. Smaller and smaller, you see. Eventually, we'll have one of everything here."

Arnaud doesn't speak. How can he?

"You seem surprised," the docent says. "I thought this is why you came—to look at this. But people come for different reasons."

Arnaud gets down on his hands and knees to look into his copy's greenish glass eyes. They seem empty at first—without a soul—then Arnaud sees something deep inside. It's another copy, he thinks, a boy in the black cave of the android's pupil, crawling there. The miniature boy is thinking of his parents who sit above the warm bakery, waiting for him to come home. He's thinking of how he could have gone to the stables. He could have held hands with a soldier or had a night of swimming in the pond at the northern edge of the city with the miller's son. He's thinking what a fool he's been. *How many of these boys are there?* Arnaud wonders as he stares into the cave of the creature's glass eye. *How many of me?* He looks toward the docent again and realizes the boy might now, finally, be ready to give him that kiss. *It will taste like dust,* Arnaud thinks. *It will taste like something formed a thousand years ago. As all these things here are made of dust.*

"I should go," Arnaud says.

"Yes," the docent says with a faint smile. "I suppose you should try."

History of a Saint

"Clockwork automata and African beetles and tusks of the Arctic Narwhal," writes the Vicomte de Barras in a letter to his wife, "such are the artifacts found in Herr Magnus Engstrom's collection at his snowbound château. It is, my dear, an astonishing display. And yet, when finally I beheld Engstrom's centerpiece—the so-called Saint of Fribourg—it became difficult for me to consider any other object. I could not wrest my gaze from that miraculous figure. The girl is said to have perished some two hundred years ago. Her corpse, however, remains *inviolate*. She looks as though she sleeps. It seemed that she might turn her head in her glass casket, at any moment, and ask me to lift the latch."

Documents from a vault at Saint Nicholas' Cathedral report that the body described by Barras and others was unearthed in the excavation of a mass peasants' grave. Workmen knelt and prayed at the site, for it appeared they'd found a "sleeping girl" buried with the bones in the earth. Bishop Schiner of the cathedral was summoned, and after examination, declared the body to be in a rare state of miraculous *incorruption*. He ordered the remains transported to the cathedral's reliquary where he would begin a petition for canonization. It appears, however, that the corpse's presence—venerated or not—began to trouble the monks who lived in the adjoining monastery. The Fribourg Saint was said to manifest a number of disquieting phenomena. Dutifully, Bishop Schiner reported these to the high council, wondering if they bore the mark of Christian miracle. The council's answer was clear. Not more than a year later, an abrupt and unceremonious sale of the relic was made to Magnus Engstrom.

In his journal of inquiry, Engstrom records the events that transpired upon the saint's arrival at his château: "I found myself intrigued by stories of her so-called miracles," he writes, "and I was eager to begin my own experiments. An emissary of the church used a pry bar to open the crate, and I must admit that my immediate reaction was one of dismay. I thought, surely, I'd suffered a fool's sale. The girl, nestled in the straw-filled box, was most certainly alive—cheeks rouged, eyes barely shut. The emissary understood my reservations and bid me to place my hand on the girl's cheek. When I did, I found that, although her skin was supple, it was cold. I took the snood from her head and found her hair was soft, pliant. Even her fingernails had not turned brittle. She appeared entirely unmarked by time. Upon closer examination, I discovered that catgut had been used to sew the insides of the girl's lips together. It seemed even the Saint of Fribourg had not escaped the ancient and superstitious practice of sealing the mouth, ensuring the dead could not speak from the grave. When I made mention of this to the emissary, he looked grim and said it was oft best not to question old beliefs."

Ensuing pages in Engstrom's journal are devoted to a defense of his investigation into the nature of the

perhaps holy personage. At the age of thirty-five, Engstrom had everything to prove and hoped the saint could
help him finally make his name. The youngest son of
prosperous Baron de Steiger, Engstrom had suffered a
series of illnesses during childhood that put him in a
state of extreme melancholy and nervous exhaustion.
For most of his adolescence, he could tolerate neither
light nor sound and kept himself in dark and silent
rooms, warmed only by a small fire, the light of which
was muted by a heavy iron grate. It was within the confines of these rooms that he began his study of scientific
aberrations—from the Vegetable Lamb of Tartary (said
to be a mammal that sprouted from the vines of a rare
fern) to documented occurrences of human resurrection
that occurred long after that of Christ.

These early interests led to a series of failures. Engstrom attempted then to pen a Cyclopedia, in which he
wished to gather all human knowledge. The writing was
abandoned after the completion of only one volume, a
tome that was composed entirely of a lengthy description
of a rare cave-dwelling fish in Southern France. There
was also the strange episode in which Engstrom secured
a portion of his father's wealth to purchase a rural village
near Bern that had been abandoned during the plague.
Engstrom announced he would use the village to create
a replica of the Heavenly Domain as described by the
Englishman John Styron. Styron had famously suffered
a blow to the head while on a sailing vessel, which re-
sulted in an ecstatic vision of Heaven. The project was
abandoned after the Mansion of God (said to be a series
of houses within houses—each decreasing in size) was
set afire by local vandals.

Magnus Engstrom's family disapproved of his curious obsessions, and it was well known that his inheritance was left in a precarious state if he could not appease his father and become a gentleman of some substance. The cabinet of wonders at the snowbound château was Herr Engstrom's desperate attempt at claiming legitimate status and repairing his name. He modeled his cabinet on the *wunderkammer* of Rudolph II, endeavoring to present the world in its entirety in the space of a single room. Engstrom wished to take his cabinet to a level of extremity never before seen. "I shall soon be turning visitors away," Engstrom writes. "The aristocracy will clamor to have a look at my collection and to hear of the experiments I've performed. I will be able to charge even my own father special alms for admittance."

Engstrom's most serious failure—the one for which he was so often judged—was of a social, not scientific, nature. And it seemed even the wondrous Saint of Fribourg could not aid him in this respect. Herr Engstrom asked for the hand of seventeen-year-old Lady Margaret of Wisberg in a further attempt to please his wealthy father. Lady Margaret was a child of the age, intelligent and serene, and though her mother was against the proposed marriage, her own misguided father saw fit to comply. After a somber and candlelit wedding beneath a canopy of lilies and Edelweiss, Herr Engstrom brought Lady Margaret to the cold environs of his château at the foot of the Bernese Alps, and there he perpetrated what appeared to outsiders as a systematic neglect of her needs. He withheld even a modicum of affection, thinking only of his cabinet of wonders, leaving the château often to pursue and purchase rarities. It became clear that his sensibilities were not suited to the comforts and traditions of marriage, and his abandonment of Lady Margaret left her in a state of perpetual misery. Isolated from her family and the beautiful fields of Wisberg where she'd been raised, Lady Margaret found little to occupy her heart. She wore a dark mantle over her dresses and a gable covered her hair. She was often seen walking the lonely mountain paths above the château, gazing down at the road that led to the city of Bern—perhaps dreaming of worlds not encased in ice. When she was overcome by the tedium of her existence, Lady Margaret was known to take a lantern from the house and explore a system of tunnels in the mountain pass above the château. Children of the village took to calling her the *Gespenst*, meaning "specter," and warned each other to stay clear of her cold lantern's light. In a letter to her mother, Lady Margaret herself writes, "If I cannot find peace in my own house, at least there is the house of the Earth to soothe me. Children watch for me in the caves, thinking I am to be feared, and perhaps they should fear me. I will become an illustration for them—so they might not suffer a fate similar to my own."

Lady Margaret was ordered by her husband not to enter the cabinet of wonders, as such scientific endeavors were perceived as unfit for the attentions of women. But on one icy winter's day when Herr Engstrom was, once again, absent from the château, Lady Margaret forced a weak-willed servant to open the door to the wonder room. She'd heard rumors about a dead girl in a glass box and wanted to see for herself if such rumors were true. In her personal journal, Lady Margaret describes the scene: "Among all the awful glass-eyed chicanery and the various depictions of the physically deformed, I found *her*. Though I expected the girl's presence to be frightening or grotesque, it was quite the opposite. A blessed calm came over me, and my first thought was that she looked like my own mother. The girl in the box had a clean and healthy face, as though she was familiar with country work. It's strange to say, but I was pleased to see such a face. I'd been surrounded for so long by the jaundiced visages of wealth. I dismissed the servant, and opened the lid of the box, so I could touch the gentle girl within. And it was when I put my hand on her own folded hands that chords of strange music drifted toward me—as if the girl was singing. I drew my hand back, waiting for her eyes to open, knowing I might faint were she to do so. But the saint remained still. I touched her again and listened to the music that emanated from her body—a heavenly song. I wondered if the girl might be filled up with angels. Finally, I grew drowsy from listening. I said a prayer and kissed her on the cheek before taking my leave of the cabinet. I hope kissing her was not too bold a thing, for hers was indeed a holy presence."

Documents regarding the sale to Magnus Engstrom make it clear that the body's sainthood was never officially decreed. According to papal law, incorruption could have a variety of possible causes, not all of them wholesome. Remarks were even made regarding the will of demons. Offices of the Canon in Rome believed Bishop Schiner had been hasty in his petition, and the bishop himself eventually agreed. He includes in his tract a list of priests who abandoned the monastery due to the presence of the Saint of Fribourg, all of them men of good standing. In an addendum, he also discusses the phenomena surrounding the body. These occurrences appear in two distinct categories. In the first are her *cu-*

rative properties. The Fribourg Saint was said to possess the power to reinvigorate spoiled fruit, meat, and plant life. If given a sufficient amount of time, her presence could restore organic matter to its original vitality. Her second power was more ambiguous and, according to the bishop, more troubling. Apparently, she was known to cause visions. "The brothers have experienced every sort of poisonous dream since the coming of the incorrupt body," writes Bishop Schiner. "They have described nights full of talking wolves and dancing women. They have seen an absence in the starlit sky where God should be. One of our most stalwart brethren even described a dream in which he rose from his bed, went to the reliquary, and held the dead girl against his own body. He says the warmth of his flesh *awakened* her, and she attempted to speak to him though her mouth appeared sealed shut. He is glad the girl could not speak, as he believes she aimed to enchant him."

Magnus Engstrom did not fear the saint's purported abilities, and he began his experiments almost immediately upon his taking possession of her. He writes: "I was skeptical to say the least regarding the phenomena surrounding the Fribourg Saint. Men of the cloth often exaggerate such happenings due to their solitude and religious fascination. I set out to test the girl myself, using scientific principles of observation. On our first evening together, I placed a shriveled plum on the saint's breast. It is said that spoiled fruit revives in her presence. I invited several persons to the cabinet the next morning to examine the plum along with me—these included the esteemed Alaric Glaus and Lucillius of Ghent. I was astonished to see that the plum had regained some of its color and did, in fact, seem less desiccated than on the previous evening. My comrades were incredulous, claiming I might have replaced the plum during the night, so I invited them to repeat the experiment and stand guard. We placed the same plum on the breast of the saint for a second night, and the next morning, my near exhausted friends found that the plum had regained a full state of freshness. When we cut the fruit open, its flesh was unmarred by decay, and when we tasted it, it was sweet."

Engstrom records a number of other such experiments. The saint revived a dying fern and was also able to cure a sick stable hound. The dog was locked in the cabinet overnight, and a terrible howling came from the room. None of the servants dared open the door. They expected to find the dog dead the next morning for all the awful noise it made, but instead they found it rejuvenated and twice as fast at catching rats.

These findings pleased Herr Engstrom, but he was not yet satisfied. Bishop Schiner had already documented similar occurrences, after all. In order to make a name for himself and to be seen as a true man of science, Engstrom needed to discover something new and definitive regarding the saint. "I shall endeavor to take my experimentation a step further than the bishop's own," he writes. "I will determine whether the saint can also heal *herself*. In doing so, I believe I may well begin to discern the very nature of the saint's incorruption."

No record indicates how Lady Margaret became aware of her husband's experiments. Perhaps it was from the gossip that was prevalent at the House of Engstrom. In her diary, Lady Margaret writes: "I care not a thing for hounds or plums. I know only how the blessed girl makes my own body feel. She raises my spirits, fills me with a joy I have never before experienced. I find I cannot stay away from her. I sit with her when Magnus is gone, and she sings for me. The music nurtures. It enlivens. I wonder what color her eyes would be if she were to open them. I like to think they would be not a single shade, but rather a complicated mix of watery blues and earthy greens."

The joyful tone of Lady Margaret's journal darkens when she discovers the nature of Herr Engstrom's future experiments. "I have learned that Magnus wishes to cut open my poor lady's *foot*," writes Lady Margaret. "He tells his awful companions (Glaus and Lucillius) that he will make a small incision between her toes. He wants to see if she can heal herself. The thought of him testing my lady in this manner is abhorrent. Let him do what he will to me, but he mustn't disturb her. She cannot leave this house even to walk the mountain paths. Her songs have grown mournful, for she too seems to know of his intentions. I must come to her aid, even if such action presents personal danger. . . . When Magnus left this evening to meet with his men at a tavern, I went directly to the cabinet. I've stolen the key from a servant so that I may come and go as I please. I sat with my lady and listened to her weeping song, attempting to console her. I confessed that I could not physically thwart my husband, but I would do whatever else was in my power to stop him.

"I do not know when her lament became a lullaby, but soon enough, I could not hold my own eyes open and fell asleep there, lying next to the bier where the glass box rests. In a dream, I saw my lady slip from her glass case like some lovely white shadow, and she came to nestle next to me on the stone floor. Her eyes were still closed. She ran her cold fingers through my hair and touched my cheeks, as I have seen the blind do. And then my lady made a magnificent gesture. She gave me the gift I'd hoped for since the moment I first saw her exquisite form—she opened her eyes. Their color was not the bluish-green I expected. No, they were a stark and shining white—like the eyes of a marble statue—with a hard black pupil cut from the center of each. Still, I was not afraid. As she held me, she began to weep. Her tears were white as milk. I kissed those white tears from her cheeks, and they turned my tongue and throat and stomach cold. From those tears a new resolve rose up in me. I pray that my poor and inelegant soul proves strong enough to do what I must."

Lady Margaret's journal grows silent for a period of three days after her experience in the cabinet. When her narrative resumes, it appears she is forcing the rigid script onto the page. "Despite my best intentions, I could not stop him. I could not stay my husband's hand. Magnus locked me in our bed chamber for hours because I would not cease my berating of him and his awful experiments. He said the saint was no business of mine. He'd purchased her from the bishop and would do with her as he pleased. There was a look in his eyes that made me wonder if he might harm me. He is a fool, of course, but perhaps a dangerous one, for he believes strongly in his convictions. That evening, he made the incision in the saint's foot, between her first and second toe, while Alaric Glaus and Lucillius looked on. My lady's music turned to a scream as he cut her, and I could hear her voice beating against every stone in the house. I hoped she might bring the whole of the château down on our heads to punish us all for Magnus's desecration. I feel ashamed to be his wife. I know I must take a more extreme course of action, and certainly I must be quick. There is talk that Magnus intends to perform a further surgery. I can barely write this—he wants to examine my poor lady's vital organs. Her heart and her liver. For whatever mad reason, he wishes to see if they too remain incorrupt."

The incision between the toes of the saint did not heal as Magnus Engstrom expected. Nor did it bleed or fester. His writings become frustrated, as he wonders how the saint cannot heal herself if she can heal so much else. It is this frustration that precipitates his need to view the body's internal organs. He wishes to learn the extent of the incorruption—is the Fribourg Saint merely a shell, and if not, what inhabits her interior? Is her still heart as perfect as her flesh? Engstrom notes Lady Margaret's unnatural attachment to the body as well: "I fear that the presence of the saint in our household is causing my wife to have nervous attacks, as I myself was once known to have. I refuse to remove the body from the cabinet; it is possible that my wife shall simply be removed from the house instead. While drunk last evening at the tavern, Alaric Glaus suggested poisoning. The comment was meant to be humorous, of course. But I have begun to wonder if there is a substance that will not kill Lady Margaret but render her ill enough that she will be forced into some warmer climate where she can convalesce. In any case, I will not let her ruin my opportunities with the Fribourg Saint."

What occurs next is beyond the full comprehension of this record. The final events surrounding the body of the Fribourg Saint caused Magnus Engstrom to impose exile upon himself. He lived out his days far from his home, on an island off the coast of Italy. The house on the island was utterly bare, washed clean by salt from the sea. It was so unlike his decorated cabinet at the château. He was said to sit in a wooden chair and look toward the water. When asked if he felt remorse over what had happened to his young and pretty wife, Engstrom merely shook his head, and said, "I do not know what happened to Margaret. No one can know such a thing."

Lady Margaret's final journal entry is fragmented, written in haste, perhaps in one of the caves above the mountain pass. The journal itself, chewed by the teeth of an animal, was discovered by a shepherd in a field beyond the château. "When Magnus took his leave, I acted. A new song filled the house, a cacophonous symphony. It might have driven me mad had I allowed it. How was it possible that only I could hear her songs? I went to the cabinet, bringing with me the milk cart that the servants use to carry milk between the barn and the main house. My lady was heavy, her joints stiff. I overturned the awful glass coffin and scattered the scarab beetles while trying to free her. Glass panes broke when the coffin's corner struck the floor. I put my lady in the milk cart, careful as I could be. I kissed her, asking forgiveness.

"No servant attempted to stop me as I left the château. They understood something had gone wrong when Magnus cut my lady's foot. They feared the woman in the box. Some of them who attend services at the cathedral have encountered rumors that the Fribourg Saint's body is inhabited by a demon. Only God and the Devil can ignore the arrow of time, they say. Such thoughts are foolish, of course, and peasantlike. I put on a pair of Magnus's fur boots and my own mantle for warmth. I pulled the milk cart through the snow toward the cave where I sometimes went to escape the confines of the house. It was my intention to keep my lady there until a carriage passed by on the road below. I would signal to the carriage with my lantern, and my lady and I would go together to the walled city of Bern. Perhaps I'd make a place there where she could be celebrated by all—not a stale museum as Magnus created, but a *shrine*. Yet no carriages appeared. The sun began to sink lower in the western sky, and I felt the bite of winter's cold there in the cave. No one would travel the road during the night, and I would have to suffer until morning.

"My lady sang to me in thankful, warming chords. I pressed my body to hers and fell in and out of restless sleep. In a dream, I put my lips against her own soft lips and discovered the reason she could not sing through her mouth. Her delicate lips had been sealed with some form of strong black string. I pulled at the string, breaking the fibers loose, stitch by stitch. When her mouth was free, my lady's jaw fell open and she released such a glorious song, finally able to use her own voice once again.

"I was so pleased to hear the vibrant music fill the cave. She told me her history in song—how she'd been born in Fribourg to a good mother and a good father. She'd been careful with her life, never acting foolishly, never eliciting her parents' scorn. Then one day, she met a man in her father's field beyond the village. She and the man walked together in the green wheat, and she did not fear him. His eyes were gentle, and his words were kind. When the two of them sat together by a stream, the man revealed to her that he was not a man at all. He was an incarnation of the Holy Ghost. Being a girl of some intelligence, she did not believe him immediately and asked that he prove himself by giving her a blessing. He dipped his hand in the stream and let her drink cool water from his palm. As she drank, he put his hand over her mouth and then over her nose. He pressed his hand firmly upon her, stopping her breath, and despite her struggling, he would not release her. He said she had been good for all her days, and she would be good for all of time. As I pictured this, I could not help but think of Magnus touching her with his terrible hands. I thought of all the cruelties he perpetrated in his prison of a house. My lady said she died there by the stream, left to wonder if she was full of the Spirit or simply full of water from a murderer's palm.

Following this passage, there is an omission in the journal, though it is not clear if the omission is due to damage from weather or because Lady Margaret became physically unable to write. The ink grows splotched and eventually an excess of it runs in dark lines down the page. How long she was in the cave remains unknown. Temperatures in the region certainly become life-threatening on winter nights. Yet, at least for a time, Lady Margaret survived. The final words in the journal are written in what appears to be a new style of handwriting, plainer and more decisive than Margaret's previous script. "I wonder now—am I sleeping or am I awake? Did I leave the dream of death where my lady died by the stream, or have I discovered some state between consciousness and reverie? The cave is dark. The oil is nearly gone from my lantern. When last I reached for my lady's hand, I felt only loose bones. Yet I do not despair, for she isn't gone. I can still hear her song. It echoes magnificently off the cave walls, so loudly that I wonder, at times, if I might be singing it myself. In any case, I know what I must do. I will gather her bones inside the folds of my mantle and leave the cave under night's cover. Magnus will not see. I'll make my way past the walls of the castle, through the snow. And eventually I'll find a good place for burying. I won't be leaving her in the ground though. She'll never be in the ground again, for when next I approach a looking-glass, I will not see my own eyes, plain and blue, reflected back. Instead, they are sure to be a revelation.

Notes on Inversion

From *Psychopathia Sexualis*, Doctor Krafft-Ebing. Vienna, Austria 1886.

Case 135.

V. was very talented. He learned easily and had a most excellent religious education. At a young age, he began to masturbate without instruction. Later in life, he recognized the danger of this practice and fought with some success against it. Soon after, he began to rave about male statuary . . .

Imagine then a ruin. White pillars against a spectral dusk. We are in Rome, Palatine Hill. Here is Flavius, done in marble. Note his musculature: swollen pectorals, firm abdominis. His cock is, of course, uncircumcised. See the flaccid shaft curled against full testes, a thatch of pubic hair. Flavius has no head, no face. It doesn't matter. We can invent such things for him. Adonian curls, high forehead, aquiline nose. Perhaps there is a cleft in his chin. His lips are full, nearly pouting.

Imagine now brushing against Flavius
in a darkened hall. We excuse ourselves,
politely. We nearly continue on our way.
Then we realize just how lovely—how
ancient. We take Flavius down from his
pedestal. We bring him to our bed. His
alabaster flesh is hard and cold. His body
is so heavy it nearly breaks the bedframe.
Imagine kissing those stony lips. Rubbing
our own cock against his timeworn beauty.
Flavius speaks to us. His voice is an echo.
His throat is some two thousand years old.
We can barely hear him. And we don't
know Latin. Still, we understand. Flavius
doesn't love us. He can hardly perceive
us at all. Yet he will do this thing we've
asked of him. When Flavius ejaculates, his
semen is a fine white powder.

Case 137.
*Homosexual feeling, perverse in origin. R. is sexually
excited by men's boots. Patient dreamed of handsome jockeys
wearing shining boots. Servants' boots affect him. Men of his
own position, wearing ever so fine boots, were of absolute
indifference. In the society of ladies, R. has been reserved;
dancing always tires him . . .*

He collapses at yet another gala. Gaslit
dance floor in a gilded hall. Stringed instruments play a waltz.

All around him, boots of every stripe:
Dealer and Jodhpur and Paddock. Tight

fitting, ankle-high. The smell of leather.
The smell of polish. Red Hessian with
golden tassels, fronds brushing his upturned face. Woolen Valenki. Top Boots.
Black Billy Boots, handsome and vital.
He likes a painted wooden heel, a scuffed
sole. He pictures men walking for miles.

He drags himself across the dance floor,
wanting to slide his tongue up a boot
shaft, investigate the delicate stitchery,
dislodge a bit of dirt. He wants to kiss
the backstay, the mulc ears, the toe box.
There is something ecstatic here, something magnificent.

He knows this is embarrassing. That's the
point, isn't it?

Case 141.

*X. believes himself to be the martyr Saint Sebastian.
He saw a painting in a gallery—a naked young man pierced
through by arrows. X. became, in a word, possessed.*

Each of my wounds is a mouth. It attempts
to swallow a sword. I am tied to an alder
tree, wrists bound. The lashings are Roman leather, knotted by soldiers I once
called friends: Atilius, Gnaeus, Sabinus.
Springtime blossoms burst from branches
above my head. My blood trickles down
the dark trunk. I am the fantasy, trussed.
Exemplary sufferer.

In the prisons of Emperor Diocletian, I
fell in love with two men, my cellmates:
Marcellian, who was large and rough (like
an animal) and Marcus who was lithe and
had a beautiful face. Every night, in the
space of our small cell, I brought these
men to Christ. My body was sweeter, they
said, than any communion wine. More
fortifying than any host. Together, we rein-
vented the Trinity. A wheel aflame in the
catacombs. When we finished our nightly
Mass, we lay together in the dust. We
caressed each other until morning light.

On the day of my execution, the sky was no
color I could name. There was a wind from
the north. The black branches of the alder
tree creaked above. My lovers were both
murdered. Dragged behind horses. Marcellian's head came off. Soldiers tied me to a
tree. They surrounded me in a half-circle
and took turns shooting arrows. Shafts,
buried in my flesh. The soldiers laughed.
They talked of other things. "This doesn't
mean I don't still love you," I whispered,
so softly no one could hear. They did not
know they were making a saint of me.

Case 146.
*Two persons in Vienna are examples. One is a barber
who calls himself "French Laura"; the other is a butcher who
calls himself "Helen" . . .*

Good day to you! Good day. (Fans flutter. Bosoms rise.) This is a knitting circle in which no knitting is done. Instead of needles we have cocks. Instead of yarn we have our slippery orifices.

Aunt Patricia has baked yet another of her delicious cakes. We remark on it with enthusiasm. There is time for gossip then. Vicki has been up to her notorious tricks. And you mustn't start us talking about Anne. We adjust our skirts and ask about the new charitable concerns. We support the Cripples' Home, The Temporary House for Lost Dogs, and, of course, The Female Society.

What items will we donate this year to the jumble sale? We can spare nearly everything. And then there is cycling. It's ever so popular these days. All the women in the park, pedaling about: Fanny and Ruth and Florence. But those uncomfortable leather bicycle seats. They have bruised us! Speaking of uncomfortable: here comes the duchess now. Look at her, will you? Just look at her.

Case 149.
He never felt nausea at the penis of others . . .

The causes of nausea: Perambulators. Light novels. Hoop skirts. Bourgeois work ethic. Portraiture. The Resurrection. The language of flowers. The children's hour. Quakers. Realism. Naturalism. Strindberg. Strindberg! Allspice pudding. The unfashionable clubs. Muttonchops.

Case 170.

The hypnotic suggestions are as follows:

1. *I abhor onanism. It makes me weak, miserable.*
2. *I no longer have a lustful inclination toward men. A man's love of other men is against religion, nature and law . . .*

We place our hand over the doctor's mouth, silencing him. We tell him we will finish this. Who are we to speak? We are all of them, we say. Every last one.

Begin the session again:

1. We will not imagine a quiet hillside in the country where men can be together unhindered. We will not imagine these men taking off their shirts in the tall grass, revealing the sort of physiques that shepherds once had. We will not imagine these men then kissing one another on the chest and on the mouth. We will not imagine them unlacing their tight brown trousers. We will not imagine them building houses there on the hillside where they can live amongst

one another. We will not imagine how they don't pray to any gods. We will not imagine how they talk at night around great campfires, faces bright, telling the old stories. Because now there are old stories to be told.

Acknowledgments

Thank you to the editors of the publications in which the following stories first appeared:

Altered States Anthology: "Night Is Nearly Done";
The Collagist: "Versailles, 1623";
Conjunctions: "The Re'em";
Diagram: "Notes on Inversion";
The Fairy Tale Review: "History of a Saint";
Fifth Wednesday: "Petit Trianon";
Hayden's Ferry Review: "Homunculus";
Hobart: "Swaingrove";
Kenyon Review: "Sodom and Gomorrah";
Knee-Jerk Magazine: "Poet and Underworld";
Law and Disorder Anthology: "The Rite of Spring";
Ninth Letter: "Metempsychosis";
The Portland Review: "The Coil";
Sequestrum: "Hydrophobia";
Vestiges: "Sleep and Death."

My gratitude to Peter Conners for his continued support of my work and to Eleanor Jackson who provides invaluable guidance at every turn. For their thoughts on the stories in this collection and for their enduring friendship, I'd like to thank Brian Leung, Scott Blindauer, Gabriel Blackwell, Chrissy Kolaya, Colin Meldrum, Christine Sneed, Tyler Pottebaum, Mike Bailey, and Josh Hoffman. Thank you to my family, especially my mother, Denise Skevington, and my father, Michael McOmber. Thank you to Chris Baugh for helping me find the energy and spirit to complete this collection. And finally, thank you to Cal Burton for his constant encouragement and love.

About the Author

Adam McOmber is the author of *The White Forest: A Novel* (Touchstone, 2012) and *This New & Poisonous Air* (BOA Editions, 2011). His work has appeared in *Conjunctions*, *Kenyon Review*, and *Diagram*. He teaches and writes in Los Angeles.

BOA Editions, Ltd. American Reader Series

No. 1 *Christmas at the Four Corners of the Earth*
Prose by Blaise Cendrars
Translated by Bertrand Mathieu

No. 2 *Pig Notes & Dumb Music: Prose on Poetry*
By William Heyen

No. 3 *After-Images: Autobiographical Sketches*
By W. D. Snodgrass

No. 4 *Walking Light: Memoirs and Essays on Poetry*
By Stephen Dunn

No. 5 *To Sound Like Yourself: Essays on Poetry*
By W. D. Snodgrass

No. 6 *You Alone Are Real to Me: Remembering Rainer Maria Rilke*
By Lou Andreas-Salomé

No. 7 *Breaking the Alabaster Jar: Conversations with Li-Young Lee*
Edited by Earl G. Ingersoll

No. 8 *I Carry A Hammer In My Pocket For Occasions Such As These*
By Anthony Tognazzini

No. 9 *Unlucky Lucky Days*
By Daniel Grandbois

No. 10 *Glass Grapes and Other Stories*
By Martha Ronk

No. 11 *Meat Eaters & Plant Eaters*
By Jessica Treat

No. 12 *On the Winding Stair*
By Joanna Howard

No. 13 *Cradle Book*
By Craig Morgan Teicher

No. 14 *In the Time of the Girls*
By Anne Germanacos

Colophon

BOA Editions, Ltd., a not-for-profit publisher of poetry and other literary works, fosters readership and appreciation of contemporary literature. By identifying, cultivating, and publishing both new and established poets and selecting authors of unique literary talent, BOA brings high-quality literature to the public. Support for this effort comes from the sale of its publications, grant funding, and private donations.

The publication of this book is made possible, in part, by the support of the following individuals:

Anonymous x 3
Gwen & Gary Conners
Angela Bonazinga & Catherine Lewis
Dr. James & Ann Burk, *in memory of Jack Sheehan*
Peter Conners
Gouvernet Arts Fund
Sandi Henschel
Christopher Kennedy
X.J. & Dorothy M. Kennedy
Jack & Gail Langerak
Dan Meyers, *in honor of J. Shepard Skiff*
Boo Poulin
Rochester LGBT Giving Circle
Deborah Ronnen & Sherman Levey
Steven O. Russell & Phyllis Rifkin-Russell
Bernadette Weaver-Catalana